A Choice of Evils

An Andrew Basnett Mystery

E. X. FERRARS

DOUBLEDAY

New York   London   Toronto   Sydney   Auckland

PUBLISHED BY DOUBLEDAY

a division of Bantam Doubleday Dell Publishing Group, Inc.
1540 Broadway, New York, New York 10036

DOUBLEDAY and the portrayal of an anchor with a dolphin are
trademarks of Doubleday, a division of Bantam Doubleday Dell
Publishing Group, Inc.

Library of Congress Cataloging-in-Publication Data

Ferrars, E. X.
A choice of evils: an Andrew Basnett mystery/E.X. Ferrars.
p.   cm.
I. Title.
PR6003.R458C46   1997
823'.912—dc20   96-34823
CIP

ISBN 0-385-48039-3
Printed in the United States of America
January 1997
First Edition in the United States of America

1   3   5   7   9   10   8   6   4   2

CHAPTER 1

The 3.45 to Gallmouth arrived at the station at 3.55, on Friday, the fifteenth of October, only ten minutes late. Most of the passengers on the train were pleasantly surprised. Professor Andrew Basnett, who had been dozing in his seat, came to himself with a start, grabbed his suitcase and the copy of the *Financial Times* which he had been reading earlier, hoping, though as usual failing, to make out if he was a little richer or a little poorer than he had been when he had last studied this newspaper, got to his feet in a hurry and made for the exit from the carriage.

On the platform he did not waste time looking for a porter but set off down the stairs to the station yard. When he and his wife Nell, who had been dead now for over ten years, had first discovered Gallmouth, there would have been more than one porter eager to carry his suitcase, and also there would have been flowerbeds on the platform. But these, like the porters, had long disappeared. In the yard, however, in the old days there would have been only two, or at most three, decrepit taxis waiting hopefully for passengers, whereas now there were more than half a dozen. You lose a little, gain a little with the passage of time, Andrew reflected. He took the taxi at the head of the rank and asked to be driven to the Dolphin Hotel.

Andrew was in his mid-seventies. He was a tall man who would have looked even taller than he generally did if he had resisted a tendency to stoop which had developed

5

during the last year or two. He had kept his spare figure and still walked with some vigour, had bony features, short grey hair and grey eyes under eyebrows that had remained formidably dark. He had an intelligent face, though its expression during the last few years had been becoming increasingly detached, instead of showing the lively interest in most things that it had had when he was younger. He had been a professor of Botany in one of London University's colleges for nearly twenty years, but now had been retired for some time, yet was still living in the flat in St John's Wood where he and Nell had lived together until her death from cancer. He had nearly moved out then, thinking of something that would not be haunted by memories. But in fact it had been the memories that had held him. Any thought of moving into something smaller and perhaps more convenient had passed long ago.

The Dolphin Hotel was on the seafront of Gallmouth. It was an undistinguished but reasonably comfortable place which suited Andrew, because, among other virtues, it was moderately inexpensive. The service was good, the food tolerable, and without being ostentatious about it, catered mostly for elderly people. Andrew and Nell had stayed there together two or three times, and now, when a need to escape from London occasionally came to him, he generally returned to their old haunt, because it was less trouble to pick up the telephone and fix up a room for himself there, knowing exactly what he would get, than to venture into the unknown.

It was a Victorian building, which only recently had improved its plumbing, installing a bathroom for each bedroom, and arranging adequate parking space in what had once been its garden. Not that parking space was of any interest to Andrew, who did not own a car, holding that to do so in London was a costly inconvenience. If it was essential to have one for some particular occasion, it could always be hired. He was thinking, as the taxi drove him to the Dolphin, that perhaps he would hire one for the week that he intended to stay in Gallmouth. On the other hand, walking would do him good and there were some attractive walks along the cliffs that rose steeply on each side of the little town.

Once comfortably installed in his room at the hotel, he treated himself to some afternoon tea. This was something that he never did when he was by himself in his flat, but to have it now in the roomy and not overcrowded lounge with its pleasant view of the sea, gave him an agreeable sense of luxury. A nice-looking girl brought him his tea on a tray, and pushed a trolley up to him laden with a variety of the rich-looking sort of cakes that he would never have thought of buying for himself at home. Something that looked soft and creamy, topped with chocolate, seemed to him particularly inviting, and gave him a sense, as he bit into it, that he really was on holiday.

Not that it could really be said that he needed a holiday. Ever since he had finished writing his life of Robert Hooke, the noted seventeenth-century microscopist, he had been unable to settle down seriously to any other work. It had been a great mistake to finish the book. He had been very contented, working at it and really, in his heart, had never believed that it would ever come to an end. But he had been tempted by a clever young editor in a large firm of scientific publishers, who had given him two or three excellent lunches and dangled a contract before him. Having a contract had made Andrew feel rather grand. Whether the fact that the editor had once been a student of his, who had gone into publishing instead of into research or teaching, had had anything to do with Andrew's finally producing the book on which he had worked happily for so long, he was not sure, but the thing was done now, and in the last month or so he had even finished the proofs, the bibliography and the index. That had been quite hard work, so perhaps, after all, he did deserve a holiday. Looking dreamily at the sea, glinting in the pale October sunshine, and eating the creamy, squashy thing that he had chosen from the trolley, he felt that it was very nice to be back in the Dolphin.

When he had finished his tea he set out for a walk along the seafront. There was a slight breeze blowing in from the sea, making the air cool, but the sunlight had not yet begun to fade into dusk. There was a sparkle on the little waves that slid in towards the beach, and on the frill of surf that toppled gently over on to the shingle. There were not many people about. The season had come to an end at least a month ago, indeed in another two or three weeks half the hotels in Gallmouth would close down for the winter. Andrew had booked in at the Dolphin just in time.

He strolled slowly along the esplanade which stretched from the base of the cliff that rose on one side of the town, to that of the one that rose on the other. One or two streets branched off it, leading to the shops, the cinema, the church, the library, a small theatre and the town hall. Andrew walked almost to the far end of the paved walk, to the point where a bridge crossed the Gall, the little river that had given the town its name and beyond which, if he wanted to go on, he would have to start climbing up the cliff there. But he did not feel like doing that. Instead, he turned into a small shopping mall where he vaguely remembered from his last visit that there was a delicatessen. He wanted to buy some cheese.

Not that the Dolphin would not have supplied cheese if he wanted it at dinner, but he had the slightly eccentric habit of eating cheese with his breakfast. Some years ago a friend who was a respected dietician had persuaded him that the day ought always to be started with some protein, and to get himself some cheese, Andrew had found, was so easy compared even with boiling an egg that he had agreed to give the theory a trial. By now, though he had no faith whatever in the health-giving properties of cheese at breakfast, he had let it become a habit and never felt that the day had properly begun till he had had a slice of it.

He was right about the delicatessen. It was where he had remembered it. He went in, bought a quarter of a pound of double Gloucester and emerging, took a look at the window of the shop next door. It was a bookshop. It had two windows, with a doorway between them. The nearer window, at which he looked first, held what seemed to be a display of children's books written by a woman called Mina Todhunter. The name stirred a memory in Andrew, not of his own childhood, when Beatrix Potter had fulfilled all his literary needs, but of a much later time, when he had often been driven into reading aloud to a nephew of his, aged four, whose favourite writer had been Mina Todhunter. The central character in all her works was a scarecrow, who wore a battered top hat, a red muffler and a tail coat and carried an umbrella, and was called Mr Thinkum. Andrew did not believe that his nephew had ever seen a real scarecrow, and he was certain that the children of the modern age had never done so, so it seemed surprising in a way that the window of a bookshop should be filled with works about one. He wondered if they had been selling well for all those years, or if this display betokened a revival. He felt almost inclined for a moment to go into the shop and buy one of the books, to see if he could discover what the writer's magic had been, but instead he moved on towards the farther window.

'Andrew!'

He started and turned.

There was the nephew, Peter Dilly, of whom he had been thinking only a moment before, who was now thirty-five and who happened to be a very successful writer of science fiction.

'Peter! What on earth are you doing here?' Andrew exclaimed.

'I might ask you that,' Peter Dilly said.

He was a small man with fair hair, pink cheeks, an attractive smile and a light, springy way of walking. His writing had made him a rich man, and since he owned a cottage of considerable charm in the country and an apartment in Monte Carlo, it was surprising to find him loose in a place like Gallmouth, unless perhaps he had come to visit friends or had some mysterious professional commitment there.

This was the case, as he explained, when Andrew repeated his question.

'Haven't you heard of the Gallmouth Arts Festival?' he asked. 'I'm speaking tonight. That isn't by any chance what's brought you, is it?'

'To hear you speak?'

Andrew had a great deal of affection for his nephew, but it would never have occurred to him to go out of his way to hear him speaking on a platform, presumably about his work, which in spite of that genuine affection, Andrew never read.

'No, no, I mean the festival,' Peter said. 'It's not much of a thing, but I was invited to speak and at the same time to stay for the weekend with someone who rather interests me and I'd nothing else to do for the moment, so I came. But you haven't answered my question. I never thought of you as likely to be interested in a thing like an arts festival.'

'I'm afraid I've got to admit that I'd never even heard of it,' Andrew replied. 'Haven't you ever heard me talk of Gallmouth? I've been coming here for the odd week or so for the last dozen years. I've just finished a job of work correcting proofs and so on, on my poor old Robert Hooke, and I thought I'd treat myself to some relaxation.'

'Yes, now that I think of it, of course I've heard you

talk about Gallmouth,' Peter said. 'I'm being stupid. But since you're here, and there actually is a festival, do you think I could persuade you to come and listen to me?'

'When would that be?'

'This evening at eight o'clock in the Pegasus Theatre. Where are you staying?'

'In the Dolphin, as usual.'

'Yes, of course. Well, I could pick you up and take you along. I assume you haven't a car.'

'No, I haven't.'

'Oh, do come, Andrew.' Peter sounded genuinely eager.

'Well, perhaps, if you want me to,' Andrew said. 'But what are you going to talk about? I didn't know you'd added public speaking to your other talents.'

'I haven't, that's the trouble.' Peter laughed. 'I've hardly ever opened my mouth in public before, and I'm as nervous as a cat on hot bricks. Not that I'm actually going to have to say a lot. There are going to be three of us on the platform, and we're each going to give a short talk on our own line of work, and how we came to choose it, and that sort of thing. Then the audience, if there is one, will sling questions at us, the thought of which doesn't much frighten me, because they're always the same. I've answered them a dozen times. Then I believe we drink coffee and then we go home. I've written my talk, of course, and only have to read it, so I shouldn't have let myself get worked up about it. But you know what a nervous character I am.'

Andrew did not believe for a moment in Peter's nervousness. He was probably looking forward with great satisfaction to the thought of appearing on a platform and hearing himself speak.

'Who are the other two who are going to be appearing with you?' he asked.

'Well, good old Todhunter, for one.' Peter said. 'She'll be talking about writing for children.'

11

'Todhunter – Mina Todhunter!' Andrew pointed at the shop window full of her works. 'You mean this lady, whose stories I used to have to read to you when you were an infant. Is she still alive? She must be very old.'

'I shouldn't think she's much more than seventy,' Peter said, 'if that. But take a look at what's written up there.'

He moved a little way back from the window and pointed at what was written above it. Andrew looked up and saw the words Todhunter's Bookshop, there in bold black capitals on a white background.

'She owns this shop then?' Andrew said.

'Yes, and I've got to go in in a minute and speak to her,' Peter answered.

'She's a local figure?'

'Very much so.'

'And who's the third person who'll be appearing with you?'

'Simon Amory.'

'Simon Amory!' Andrew was startled. *Death Come Quickly* Amory?'

'That's right,' Peter said.

'He's a friend of yours?'

Death Come Quickly was the title of a play that had been running in the West End for two years, and that had been filmed and televised, after originally appearing, about four years before, quite modestly as a novel by an unknown author.

'Well, I know him slightly and I'm staying with him for the weekend,' Peter said.

'If he's in on this thing you're involved in this evening,' Andrew said, 'it's a little more of an event than you've just suggested.'

'Not really. He happens to live here, and when the local Arts Council decided to have authors speaking in their festival, the first thing they did, naturally, was invite him to be one of the speakers.'

'And where do you come in?' Andrew asked.

Peter took a few steps towards the second shop window, into which Andrew had not yet looked. Following Peter, he saw that the window contained a display of the works of Simon Amory and of Peter Dilly. Numbers of Peter's most successful novel, called *Whalewater*, were there. It was a story of how, by a miracle of genetic engineering, a whale had been developed that could fly as well as swim, which naturally was taken over eagerly by military Intelligence because of its remarkable usefulness in overland and underwater spying. The book had been filmed and had made a rich man of Peter.

'You see,' he said with a little smile, 'I'm not unknown.'

'Of course not,' Andrew said, 'but how did you get to know Amory?'

'We met at a Foyle's luncheon,' Peter replied, 'and this affair down here was just being organized and he seemed to think I was the sort of thing they wanted. Anyway, a few days later I got a formal invitation from the committee to speak, and an informal invitation from Amory to spend the weekend with him. I'm rather regretting it now, but at the time it sounded entertaining.'

'Why are you regretting it? Don't you like him?' Andrew asked.

Peter hesitated very slightly before he answered, 'Oh yes, I like him, but I can't make him out. He puzzles me. But now I've got to go in here and speak to Miss Todhunter. Amory suddenly decided to give a small dinner party this evening before the show and he wants me to ask her to attend. Come in with me and meet her. I haven't met her myself yet, so I can't promise you what she'll be like, but I'm sure she'll be charming. Amory seems to be devoted to her.'

Andrew laughed and shook his head.

'I'll leave her to you. And I think I'll be getting back to the Dolphin. If you have any time to spare while you're down here, telephone me there and we'll arrange to have lunch or something together. We don't normally see as much of each other as I'd like.'

'But aren't you coming to the show tonight?' Peter sounded really dismayed. 'Oh, do come, Andrew. I was sure you would.'

'Well, I'll think about it. I'll see how I feel when I've had a couple of drinks. Now I'll leave you to the lady inside. You could thank her from me for all the help she gave me with keeping you quiet when you were very young. I wonder if her Mr Thinkum had sowed the seeds in you of your great scientists in *Whalewater*.' For Mr Thinkum, like Peter's whale, using his umbrella as a sail, could fly. 'Goodbye for now.'

Andrew put a hand on Peter's shoulder for a moment, then turned to retrace his steps down the mall and the esplanade towards the Dolphin, while Peter went into Mina Todhunter's shop.

Andrew was in his bedroom at the Dolphin, thinking of going down to the bar for the two drinks of which he had spoken to Peter, when the telephone rang.

He assumed that it was Peter ringing, since no one else knew where he was, and he felt a certain gratitude for the sound because it cut across the thoughts, or rather lack of thoughts, with which he had been occupied for the last half hour. He had an unfortunate habit, when nothing else occupied his mind, of letting scraps of verse, or sometimes of songs, repeat themselves endlessly and meaninglessly in it. They were nearly always fragments which he supposed had meant something to him in his childhood and which had somehow lingered on in his brain when they had ceased to have any interest for him. If he had managed to repeat to himself lines from Shakespeare, say, or Milton, or Donne, he might, he sometimes fancied, have derived some pleasure from what he had remembered, but those, however much he venerated them, would not stay securely in his head, while he might be troubled for a whole day at a time by nursery rhymes, or commonplace jingles.

When the telephone rang he was muttering to himself some lines from the *Bab Ballads*.

> *'Among them was a bishop who*
> *Had lately been appointed to*
> *The balmy isle of Rum-ti-Foo*
> *And Peter was his name . . .'*

How many times he had repeated it since parting with Peter he had no idea, but it was irritating him deeply that he could not blot it from his mind. He snatched up the telephone and said, 'Yes?'

But it was not Peter who spoke. It was an unfamiliar voice, deeper than Peter's, smooth and rather cold, though what followed was friendly.

'Professor Basnett?'

'Yes,' Andrew repeated.

'My name's Amory,' the voice said. 'Simon Amory. Peter's told me that you're a relative of his.'

'His uncle, actually,' Andrew answered.

'And that you met by chance in the town this afternoon. I think he told you about the show we're putting on this evening, he and I and dear Mina Todhunter, and that you were going to come along to listen to us. I expect he also told you that he's staying with me and that I'm laying on a small dinner party before the event. It would give me great pleasure if you would join us.'

'That's very kind of you,' Andrew said, though he was not aware that he had actually promised Peter that he would attend the performance in the Pegasus Theatre. 'If it isn't putting you to any trouble . . .'

'None at all. We'll be delighted to have you. I'll send

the car for you. It's quite informal. Just a few friends. Well, we'll pick you up about half past six, if that's all right with you. Very early, I'm afraid, but as the show starts at eight it seemed better to be early than having to rush our drinks and our meal. I look forward to meeting you. Goodbye.'

The ringing tone sang in Andrew's ear.

He put his own instrument down and stood still for a minute, thinking over what had just happened. *Just a few friends.* He had before this accepted invitations to parties which were to consist of just a few friends and on arriving had found at least thirty people gathered together, all in evening dress. He hoped such a thing was not going to happen this evening. Following his trip from London and then his stroll about the town, he was distinctly tired and in spite of wanting to please Peter, would have preferred a quiet dinner by himself and the chance to go early to bed. However, he had committed himself now and it would be advisable, he thought, even if he was to meet only a few friends of Simon Amory, to change out of the slacks and pullover that he was wearing, and to put on the one dark suit that he had brought with him. When this was done he went downstairs and waited in the lounge for whoever it was who was coming to fetch him.

It was Peter who came and he was driving a Rolls.

When he saw Andrew admiring the car, he grinned and said, 'You didn't know I'd risen to this, did you? Nice, isn't it?'

'Is it really yours?' Andrew asked.

'Damn it, you always see through me,' Peter said. 'No, it's Simon's. I've still got my Mercedes, which is very nice too, but not in this thing's class. Well, hop in and we'll get going.'

They both got into the car and Peter turned it in front of the hotel and took it down the short drive to the gates that led out to the main street.

It was dusk and the streetlamps had all been lit. Only the sea was an expanse of darkness. Once in the street, Peter turned to the right, the road mounting a steep hill which soon left the houses behind. Between the road and the cliff-top the space was wooded with beech trees that even in the twilight it could be seen were covered in the splendid copper of autumn.

'Now, tell me what I'm actually in for,' Andrew said. 'A few friends – that can mean anything. And different people have different ideas about informality.'

'Oh, you needn't worry,' Peter said. 'I think we'll only be about half a dozen. You and I and Todhunter and Simon and the Chairman of the festival, a man called Edward Clarke, and a woman who's some sort of relation of Simon's. Her name's Rachel Rayne. She's just arrived from America and I don't know much about her.'

'Isn't Amory married?'

'He was, but she died, I think it was five or six years ago. Leukaemia, I believe. The curious thing is that he didn't start writing until after her death. I suppose it may have begun as a way of filling the gap, but with the fantastic success he had with that first book of his, I suppose it took him over, so to speak. Have you read it?'

'I'm afraid I haven't.'

'Or seen the play?'

'No. But I saw a shortened version of it on television. I doubt if it was fair to him. For one thing it said that the book was by someone else and the television version was only based on characters created by him. If I'd been him I think I'd have been fairly disgusted.'

'Well, it kept the money rolling in, I expect, so he was probably quite happy about it.'

'What did he do before he took to writing?'

'I think he was a chartered accountant.'

'Here in Gallmouth?'

'Oh no, in London. He's only lived full time in

Gallmouth for the last few years. He and his wife saw a house here when they were on a visit to friends and fell in love with it and bought it for when he retired. But she died and never lived here.'

'Peter, you said this afternoon that he puzzled you. What did you mean by that?'

Peter did not reply at once. He peered ahead of him up the road that was lit by the long shaft from the car's headlights.

Then he said, 'I said that, did I?'

'Yes,' Andrew replied.

'Well, I shouldn't have. I didn't really mean anything.'

'Oh, come on, of course you meant something. What was it?'

'I suppose I was thinking . . .' Peter paused, then went on hesitantly. 'It's probably absurd, but I can't get rid of a feeling that he dislikes me. Yet he pressed me to come down to do this show tonight, and then to come and spend the weekend with him, and he's never been anything but pleasant and friendly to me. So it's probably some feeling in myself that's worrying me. Jealousy, for instance. I've done well enough in my way, but it can't compare with what's happened to him. And because I don't like the idea that I'm capable of such cheap jealousy, I've transferred the feeling on to him.'

'Sounds complicated,' Andrew observed.

'Yet you know what I mean.'

'I suppose I do, but I've never noticed any undue signs of jealousy in your character. I'll wait and see what I make of him myself.'

'Yes, of course.' Peter had slowed the car down outside a gate in a high stone wall. The gate was open and he turned the car in at it. 'I admire him, you know, and I want to be liked by him, but I've got this queer feeling . . . Perhaps the fact is that I'm a little afraid of him.'

He drove along a drive under two tall rows of chestnuts,

18

splendidly copper-coloured like the beeches on the cliff. Andrew saw a house ahead of them, not as large as the approach to it had led him to expect, a building of only two storeys, with small windows in its stone walls and a small porch jutting out over an oaken front door. Lawns spread out to right and left of the house, with what looked like stables joined on to one end of it, and a summerhouse among some holly bushes a little way off from it on the other. There were lights in all the ground-floor windows. As the car stopped in front of the entrance the door opened.

A light was on inside and the figure that stood in the doorway was only a dark shape against it: a man, tall, very erect and slimly built, but with wide shoulders and a striking air of dignity. That was Andrew's first impression of Simon Amory. He waited in the doorway while Peter leapt out of the car and hurried round it to open the door beside Andrew and as he did so Amory came forward, holding out his hand.

'Professor Basnett?' he said. 'I'm so glad that you could come. Peter, there's no need to put the car in the garage. We'll be wanting it presently. Come in, Professor, and meet your fellow victims, the people who've been persuaded to come with us and listen to a few of us talking a great deal too much about ourselves.'

Andrew did not really see much of the other man's face until they were in the lighted hall. It was a long, narrow hall, with a steep staircase, carpeted in dark crimson, rising out of it to the floor above. The ceiling was low and dark with heavy beams. Andrew guessed that the house dated probably from the seventeenth century. The walls were white and decorated with a few flower prints. The only furniture was a bow-fronted walnut chest that had a telephone on it and a silver bowl filled with sprays of bronze leaves. At the far end of the hall was a glass door which presumably opened into the garden.

Looking at his host, Andrew saw a man of about forty-five, with a sharp-featured face, high cheekbones and hollow cheeks, a long, sharp nose and a pointed chin, a taut nervous face that wore an oddly tight-lipped smile and had bright, observant eyes. His hair was dark and curly and still plentiful. His skin was tanned to a healthy brown.

He opened one of the doors in the narrow hall and ushered Andrew in ahead of him. Andrew's first impression was that the room was full of people, but that, he realized in a moment, was merely the result of the low, dark ceiling and the great fireplace that occupied most of one wall. A fire of logs was alight in it. But he noticed that there were also a couple of discreetly placed radiators. It would be a very comfortable room in winter. The number of people waiting there was actually only three, a short, bald man of about fifty, a slim woman of perhaps thirty-five, and a square, heavily built, crop-haired woman who was probably in her seventies and who, Andrew felt sure as soon as he saw her, was Mina Todhunter.

This turned out to be right, for Simon Amory introduced her at once.

'And I don't need to tell you who Mina Todhunter is,' he said, 'for even if you were too old to have her works read to you in your infancy, I expect you often read them in your time to a younger generation. Your nephew, for instance.'

She smiled up at Andrew and in a deep, gruff voice said, 'Your nephew's told me already that he cut his teeth on them.'

She was sitting on a low sofa, close to the fire. She had a square face and a square head, covered with short, bristly grey hair. Her eyes, slightly bulging, were a pale, clear blue under thick grey eyebrows. Her lips were thick and when she smiled her mouth seemed to open right across her face, showing excellent false teeth. Her body was thick and heavy and looked powerful. She was wearing a very simple dress of red and black jersey and a pair of long, dangling earrings of black and gold plastic.

It was strange in a way, he thought, that until that afternoon, he could not remember having seen her works in any bookshop that he had visited for a very long time, and he had a feeling that if they had been there they would have caught his eye. He had mildly sentimental memories of Mr Thinkum. He had enjoyed reading about him to Peter, who was his sister's only child and Andrew's only nephew. He and Nell had had no children and Peter had always meant a great deal to them.

Simon Amory continued his introductions. 'My sister-in-law, Rachel Rayne, just home from America, after spending nearly ten years there. She was a professor of Social Anthropology in one of those Mid-Western universities, but now she's come home to a job in London.'

The young woman who was standing by one of the small windows set deep in the thick walls gave Andrew a pleasant smile and said, 'But not as a professor, as you'll understand. They're much more lavish over there with the title than we are here. Here, I'm a mere senior lecturer.'

She was on the tall side, slim and delicately made, with an oval face with neat, small features and grey eyes set far apart under finely arched eyebrows. Her hair was fair and brushed straight back from her face into a bunch of curls at the back of her head. She was wearing well-cut trousers of some heavy, dark green silk and a pale green blouse, an outfit that suited her very well. Andrew worked it out that if she was Simon Amory's sister-in-law she was probably the sister of his dead wife, unless she was the wife of a brother of his. But she had no ring on her left hand, he noticed.

'Are you performing this evening?' he asked.

'Oh, heavens, no!' she said. 'I'm no writer. Producing

21

an occasional paper is the very most I can do, and that almost kills me.'

There was a very faint trace of an American accent in her voice, acquired presumably during her ten years in the Middle West and which probably would be shed when she had had a year or two in London. It was a resonant voice, soft but very clear.

'And now let me introduce you to our Chairman,' Amory said, turning to the short, bald man who was standing by the fire. 'Edward Clarke, who's responsible for the whole show. He's Chairman of the Gallmouth Literary Society and though this is a festival of the Arts and not exclusively literary, he's seen to it that we scribblers had our fair share of time. There was a poetry reading yesterday, very successful, though the day before we had some ballet, and tomorrow we hand over to the drama people. They're doing *The Duchess of Malfi*.'

'Ah, *The Duchess of Malfi*,' the short man said. He appeared to be about fifty and had a round, red face with soft-looking, bulging cheeks and a small, red mouth which hardly moved when he spoke. His voice was thin and shrill. 'Our first idea was some comedy, some Goldsmith, perhaps – *She Stoops to Conquer*, or something like that, but then we began to feel that that's too hackneyed and that we'd go for tragedy. You know the play, of course, Professor. A wonderful thing.'

'I've seen it once,' Andrew replied. 'Wasn't it a bit ambitious for you?'

'Ah, our people aren't amateurs,' Edward Clarke said, guessing correctly that that was what Andrew had assumed. 'Professionals, every one. Our director's retired, but he'd a notable career while he was still working, and he knew how to collect the actors we needed. I saw them rehearsing yesterday afternoon. I think we can promise you a fine performance.'

'Who's the Duchess?' Andrew asked.

'A very gifted young woman — well, she isn't as young as she looks, I dare say she's seen forty — but outstandingly talented. Name of Magda Braile.'

'*Magda Braile*!'

There was a hiss of astonishment in Amory's voice, or it might have been disbelief. His eyes opened wide and shone with extraordinary brilliance.

'You said Magda Braile?' he asked.

'Yes, I know it's amazing that she was ready to take part in our modest little festival, and I realized we're extraordinarily privileged to have got hold of her —'

'I thought you'd Fran Borthwick,' Amory interrupted.

'So we had, but she's gone down with flu. That's why it's such an extraordinary bit of luck to get someone like Magda Braile to take over.'

'Oh yes, indeed!' There was sneering sarcasm in the voice and a brilliance in Amory's eyes that could only have come from violent anger. He seemed about to say something more but then with an effort to take command of himself. All he said was, 'Drinks, everybody?'

CHAPTER 2

Dinner was served by a small man in a white jacket. The dining-room faced the sitting-room across the narrow hall. Like the sitting-room it had a low, dark ceiling and it had two small windows set deep in thick stone walls. Andrew found himself sitting between Mina Todhunter, who was on Simon Amory's right, and Rachel Rayne. The table was long and narrow and dark with two or three centuries of polishing. The man in the white jacket, Andrew understood, was the husband of the cook and besides acting as butler, when it was required of him, was gardener and chauffeur. In fact, the couple ran the establishment and were regarded by Amory as the most valuable asset that wealth had brought to him.

'I've a very wonderful woman myself,' Mina Todhunter said gruffly to Andrew, 'but she only comes in once a week. She goes through my flat like a whirlwind, leaving it spotless. But I have to look after the shop almost by myself, with only a little help now and then, and I'm getting a bit stiff in the joints for coping with it. I've thought of asking my Mrs Leonard to give me a second morning, but it would be so expensive. Wages are fantastic nowadays.'

'You live over the shop, do you?' Andrew asked.

It surprised him that Miss Todhunter should be worrying about paying for two mornings from her Mrs Leonard. If her books had been selling steadily from the time when he had first become acquainted with them, at least thirty years ago, to the present time, he would have thought that she must be at least prosperous, if not actually rich.

'Yes, I've a very nice little flat there,' she replied. 'I was born there and grew up there. My father started the shop, so I had books in my blood from my infancy. Of course I haven't spent my whole life there. I was in the ATS in the war and I've travelled a certain amount. But when my father died I wanted to keep the old place going in his memory. Financially, it isn't exactly a gold mine, but I find it very interesting. One gets to know some of one's regular customers, you know, and some of them are very interesting. That's how I got to know Simon. And it's a very quiet life really, and I can get on with my writing, though I don't do much nowadays. Taste in children's reading has changed very much since television got going.'

'Has your Mr Thinkum never been televised?' Andrew asked.

She gave a little crow of laughter.

'Imagine that!' she said. 'You're a professor and you're acquainted with my Mr Thinkum! That's one of the nicest things that's happened to me for a long time.' Her slightly bulging, pale blue eyes glistened with pleasure. 'Oh, of course, you had to read them to Peter when he was a child. But to have remembered them all this time!'

'Won't you be telling us this evening how he came into existence?' Andrew said.

Amory joined in the conversation. 'Of course she will, and she'll be asked how she thought of him, and did she write her stories by hand or on to a typewriter, and how long did it take her to write one of her books, and where do her ideas come from, and who are her favourite writers of children's books, and did she take any of her plots from real life or are they all imaginary. They're the questions one always gets asked, I've found. Usually the one about the typewriter comes first. To go by my own experience, one's got to assume that it's the most important literary interest of the average reader.'

'And do you, in fact, work by hand or straight on to a typewriter?' Andrew asked. 'Or perhaps nowadays one should say a word processor.'

He thought he saw a trace of annoyance on Amory's face.

'By hand, as a matter of fact,' he said.

'Of course, getting things typed is terribly expensive,' Mina Todhunter said. 'I type most of my own work myself, though that's becoming a bit of a problem, because my back's beginning to trouble me, which also makes doing the illustrations a bit difficult. And I haven't got on to a word processor yet. I stick to my dear old electric type-writer, which seemed the most modern thing in the world when I bought it.'

From across the table Peter said, 'I've taken to dictating most of my stuff on to tape. When I tried it first I thought I'd never manage it, I felt such a fool wandering around the room, talking out loud to myself. But by degrees I began to find it rather exciting. It can feel very dramatic, specially the love scenes, though one's got to make sure they don't carry one away. Do you think perhaps I shouldn't mention that this evening?'

'You'll be the success of the evening if you do,' Edward Clarke said in his oddly high voice. 'It's true you may offend a few people, but we aren't such prudes in Gallmouth as perhaps you expect. Of course, if you can get some sex into your talk you'll do splendidly.'

'He was talking of love scenes, not sex scenes,' Rachel Rayne said. 'They aren't necessarily identical.'

'Ah well, a hint of understanding of some of the more popular perversions,' Edward Clarke said, 'as our dear Simon has understood, is a sure winner. Can't you do anything with that?'

'Not my line,' Peter said. 'My characters are all of them utterly normal. A bit mad at times, but only in a very normal way.'

Amory smiled. 'And mine, I suppose, are very sane, but in a somewhat abnormal way. I'd advise you against talking much about that sort of thing this evening, however. Stick to those questions I mentioned, and you'll be giving people what they really want.'

'Well, you should know about that, if anyone does,' Rachel said.

'You don't really approve of success, do you, dear?' Mina Todhunter said. 'So many people don't. It's really rather a pity.'

'Ah, I do, if the right people get it,' Rachel said.

There was irony in her tone, and it brought a frown to Amory's face, but he made no reply. It was soon evident to Andrew, however, as the meal continued, that there was no love lost between Amory and his sister-in-law and it made him wonder what had brought her to stay with him. It might be, of course, that during her years in America she had forgotten what he was like, supposing that they had known each other before she went there. Her sister's marriage might not have come about until after Rachel had gone away. This might be a first meeting for the two of them.

The meal was consumed rather hastily, for after all there was not a great deal of time to spare before they were due at the Pegasus Theatre. This turned out to be very small, with a tiny stage at one end and only a dozen or so rows of seats for the audience. There was also a doorway that led into a bar, in which there were tables where food of some kind seemed to be available. The place was pleasantly decorated and had a certain cosy charm. Andrew was driven there by Amory in his Rolls, together with Peter and Rachel, but the others drove in their own cars in which they had arrived earlier at Simon Amory's house. It intrigued Andrew, in view of her slightly ostentatious parade of poverty, that Mina Todhunter's car was a BMW.

They did not go into the town by the steep road up

which Peter had brought Andrew from the hotel, but along a road that took them straight into the centre of the town. It was only a few minutes' drive. The audience seemed to be trickling in at the main entrance of the theatre when they arrived, although they did not go in there, but at a door at the side of the building, which led into a space under the stage, where there were two or three small rooms, into one of which Edward Clarke, whom Andrew by now had learnt was a solicitor, besides being Chairman of the Literary Society, led the way.

There was a mirror on the wall, with a collection of what Andrew took to be materials for the make-up that the actors would be needing on the following evening spread out on a table before it, and a chair facing it on which Mina Todhunter immediately sat down to touch up her own make-up. She had a comb and a lipstick in the small black handbag that she was carrying, and ran the comb through her short grey hair, making it stand up in an even more bristly fashion than it had before, then she spread lipstick lavishly on her wide mouth. She looked pleased with the result and smiled at herself contentedly in the mirror.

Meanwhile Andrew had addressed Edward Clarke. 'Do you do this every year?'

'Good heavens, no!' Clarke replied. 'This is the first time we've ever attempted it. It's been strictly experimental. But I must say we've been very satisfied with what we've achieved. We've had good audiences every evening. We've stuck to evenings only, though another year we might include mornings and afternoons. It depends on how much publicity we get. This year we've depended on local people for our audiences, but if people showed signs of coming from some distance, even London perhaps, and filling up our hotels, we'd be more ambitious.'

'And organizing the whole thing has been in your

hands, has it?' Andrew said. 'You must have had to work very hard.'

'Ah, I can't lay claim to being the sole organizer,' Clarke replied with a laugh, which like his voice was thin and shrill. 'We've a splendid committee of very hard-working people; Mina for one.'

'And I suppose Amory is on it too.'

'Well, no, as a matter of fact, he isn't. Of course, when he came to live here we immediately invited him to be on the committee of our Literary Society, but though he's helped us from time to time he wouldn't be a member of it. I suppose he's so involved with work connected with his play and his film and all that that he hasn't got time for it. I don't blame him. He's really a public figure now-adays, and when he comes down to Gallmouth what he wants is to escape from all the attention he normally has to put up with. He and his poor wife Lizbeth used to come down here sometimes, you know, when she was alive and before he'd ever thought of writing. They used to stay with friends who lived in the house he lives in now. That's how he got to know it. The friends, Mr and Mrs McCall, left for New Zealand some time ago, and sold it to him. And although he keeps himself to himself, he's really been a great acquisition.'

'And Miss Rayne is Mrs Amory's sister, is she?' Andrew asked.

'Yes, but I don't think they ever saw much of each other,' Clarke replied. 'Miss Rayne went off to a job in America almost as soon as she'd got her doctorate at Cambridge. They were really very unlike. Miss Rayne's got such a strong personality, don't you think? Whereas Lizbeth Amory was very quiet and reserved. Very intelligent, of course. She seemed to have a great deal of understanding of other people, at least I always thought so. But she was very shy compared with her sister.'

29

'Did Miss Rayne never come over to see her sister even when she knew she had leukaemia?'

'I'm not sure. Perhaps she did. The Amorys were a good deal in London then, of course. But Miss Rayne talks as if it's ten years since she was last in this country.'

'Are you talking about me?' Rachel Rayne said, coming to stand beside Andrew. 'I seemed to hear my name.'

'Only about how long it is since you were last in England,' Clarke said. 'I was saying I thought it was ten years.'

'That's correct,' Rachel said. 'And no doubt you were saying how callous of me it was not to come when I knew my sister was dying. Well, of course it was callous. But she told me not to come, and I suppose she had her reasons. They puzzled me at the time, but as a matter of fact I understand them better now than I did then. I think she knew that Simon and I would never be exactly friends, which must sound a very discourteous thing to say about my host, but it's true all the same. He wouldn't argue about it. And all that she wanted at the end was to be alone with him. We used to write to each other occasionally and once, before she got ill, she came out to stay with me. I'm very glad she did that.'

'Didn't you know her husband then before you left for America?' Andrew asked.

'Oh, yes, she married when she was only twenty-five and I was still a student. I went to the wedding. But I can't say I really knew him. She was six years older than I was.'

A sudden cry came from the doorway. 'Simon!'

Everyone in the room turned to look towards the open door.

A small woman stood there. She looked as if she might be a little over forty, though she had the slimness and the air of vitality of someone much younger. But her face was not young and this was not because of the fine wrinkles

30

that had appeared at the corners of her eyes and her mouth. It had something to do with an air of poised self-assurance. She had abundant auburn hair and eyes of the colour that is usually called green, though it is really grey, and which had been heavily made up. Her mouth had been coloured by a very dark lipstick. She was dressed in a black trouser-suit with a bright silk scarf thrown carelessly over her shoulders. Behind her in the passage along which she had come was a man, but he did not advance into the room behind her as she came into it, but remained standing in the passage as if he did not intend to follow her.

She went straight up to Simon Amory, threw her arms round his neck and kissed him warmly on both cheeks. That it was on both cheeks made the gesture somehow a little more formal, a little more merely friendly than a single kiss on one cheek would have done. But still he made no response to it. His body had gone rigid and a look of acute irritation, or perhaps of something graver than that, had appeared on his face.

'What on earth are you doing here, Magda?' he asked harshly.

'I've come to hear you speak, of course,' she answered.

'It must be the first time you've ever thought of doing that,' he said.

'Darling, you aren't trying to pick a quarrel with me, are you?' She had linked an arm through one of his and though he did not actually push her away, he looked as if it was what he would have liked to do. 'We never quarrel, you know we don't. Now aren't you going to introduce me to your friends?'

He spoke glumly to the room at large. 'This is Magda Braile. Tomorrow's *Duchess of Malfi*, I believe.' Then he recited the names of all the people in the room. 'And what about your friend? Aren't you going to introduce him?'

The man in the passage looked as if he would have

31

preferred not to have been noticed. He had the air of being ready to turn and walk away if only he could detach the woman he was with from her old friend. For an old friend, Andrew thought, was a fairly safe description of her relationship with Amory. It might not be an adequate one, but at least he felt it could hardly be wrong.

'Oh, of course, but he's very shy,' she said. 'He doesn't really like meeting strangers. Do come in, Desmond, darling, instead of lurking in that doorway. Desmond Nicholl,' she added. 'You've probably heard of him. He's a very clever photographer. Out of sheer good nature he's going to take some photographs of the show tomorrow, and that'll help to give your festival some nice publicity. It may help you if you ever want to have another.'

The man took a step backwards into the passage, as if he were in a hurry to leave and expected the woman to follow him. He looked about the same age as she did, was tall and thin and had a pale, cadaverous face. The skin of it looked as if it were stretched a little too tightly over the bone behind it. His eyes were deep set, dark and bright. He had very little hair left, but what there was was black, and he had a well-shaped head which carried off his baldness with a certain dignity.

Edward Clarke advanced on him at once with an outstretched hand.

'Delighted to have you here, Mr Nicholl,' he said. 'If only we'd known you were coming we could perhaps have arranged some special scenes for you to photograph. We've one or two of the local photographers on the job, of course, and their work's been appearing in our press here for the past week, but someone with your reputation would be quite different.'

'Now you mustn't say that sort of thing to Desmond,' Magda Braile said. 'He'll only tell me he's sure you've never actually heard of him. Well, darling, we'd better be going up and getting our places in the hall. I'm so looking forward to hearing you speak about your writing, Simon, love. You're usually so unwilling to do it. Now, good evening, everyone, and the best of luck for the show.'

She withdrew her arm from Amory's and took that of her friend, Nicholl, and the two of them went away up the stairs that led to the auditorium.

Andrew turned to Rachel Rayne.

'Perhaps we should do that too. All the others are performing, but you and I are audience.'

'Yes, let's go,' she said.

'And we'll meet in the bar when it's all over,' Edward Clarke said. 'Don't forget that.'

'Not if that woman's going to be there,' Amory said in a bitter voice. 'My God, if I'd known she was coming I'd have . . .'

But he did not actually say what he would have done if he had known that she was to be there. Only his eyes said it for him. Andrew was glad to leave the room and climb the stairs with Rachel Rayne after the other two.

They found seats near the front of the hall. Magda Braile and her friend had settled down near the back of it. There was a fairly good audience, though there were still a number of empty seats. On the stage there were a table and four chairs and soon after Andrew and Rachel had taken their places the three writers and Edward Clarke appeared there, to be greeted by a little burst of clapping, and sat down, Mina Todhunter and Edward Clarke in the two centre seats, and Peter Dilly beside Mina and Simon Amory beside Edward Clarke. There was a pretty bowl of flowers on the table, but except for it and the chairs the stage was bare. It looked a little like an office that had closed for the night in some not very successful business.

Turning towards Andrew, Rachel spoke in a low voice. 'Do you know Simon very well?'

'I met him for the first time this evening,' Andrew replied.

'Really? You aren't an old friend?'

'No. And even my nephew Peter hasn't known him for long, and I was only invited because Peter and I met by chance in the town.'

'You don't know Mina either, then?'

'No, though I do remember her books.'

'And Simon's too?'

'No, I'm afraid I must admit that I haven't read anything of his, or seen that amazingly successful play that's been running in London for so long.'

'You really should see it,' she said. 'It's very good. It's so much better than what he's written since. I've heard it suggested that the two books he's had published since *Death Come Quickly* came out were really written before it and probably got turned down by several publishers, and they've only come out now because they think that anything with his name on it is bound to be a success. And I think they have sold fairly well, though they don't compare with the other. But I'd like to know what you make of Simon.'

'I haven't really had a chance to make anything of him yet,' Andrew said.

'But first impressions can be very interesting.'

Andrew was inclined to agree with her, but felt that there would be some discourtesy in discussing their host that evening.

'You know, he puzzles me,' Rachel went on.

It occurred to Andrew that that was just what Peter had said about Amory in the afternoon.

'He's so different from what I thought he was when he first married my sister,' she added. 'Of course, he's never liked me. I think that's one of the reasons why I stayed away so long. I used to be so fond of my sister and I couldn't bear the feeling that he'd come between us.'

Peter, Andrew remembered, had a feeling that Amory, in spite of having invited him to stay with him during the festival, did not really like him.

'Whom does Simon like?' Andrew asked.

'Oh, he's devoted to Mina. He plays chess with her every Saturday afternoon and he'll always do anything she asks.'

'How long have you been staying here?' Andrew asked.

'Only a week.'

'What brought you if you thought your brother-in-law didn't like you?'

'Oh, just a feeling that I ought to try to repair the breach —'

But at that point she was interrupted by Clarke getting to his feet and clapping his hands loudly. There was silence in the hall.

'Ladies and gentlemen, I'm not going to make a speech,' Clarke began and then went on to make one, introducing the three writers who were on the stage with him and promising that when each had given a short talk about their work, the audience would have the opportunity of questioning them on any points that had specially interested them. It ended with his asking Mina Todhunter to open the proceedings.

She stood up and began her talk by giving a loud, hoarse laugh. For some reason this evoked some laughter in the audience, at which she treated them to her wide smile.

'You may not believe me, but I began my career as a writer at the age of five,' she said. 'As soon as I could read and write, in fact, and I was taught to do that early, I took to writing stories. They were all more or less the same, and they all began, "Once upon a time there was a king, and he had twelve daughters, and their names were . . ." And then I wrote down twelve names and that was the whole story. And then I hid my little notebook, because my worst nightmare was the thought that someone might read what I'd written.'

She went on to describe how her mother had become irritated at finding notebooks hidden all over the house, particularly under the cushions of chairs in the sitting-room, and had managed to persuade her that if only she would put them in her work-basket, neither her mother nor anyone else would ever read what they contained.

'And when she was nearly ninety,' Mina said, 'she told me that though she had longed to know what I had written, she had kept her promise and never once looked inside one of my little books, or allowed anyone else to do so.'

Then she told how she had later discovered that she had a certain skill at sketching and had begun to illustrate her stories. Indeed, for a time this had been much more important to her than her writing. It was not until she was in her twenties that she had had thoughts of publication and for a time she had met with no success. But then, and she did not know how it had happened, Mr Thinkum had emerged in her consciousness. She did not believe that she had ever seen a real scarecrow, busily about his work in some field, yet he had come to her as a complete individual, most probably, she thought, from some picture book that she had possessed in her own childhood but had since forgotten. And Mr Thinkum, for a time, had been a best-seller. Her trouble was, however, that she had grown tired of him, her stories had become mechanical, her illustrations lifeless. She had attempted something more ambitious, but in this she had failed, and so, accepting her own limitations, she had from time to time sent Mr Thinkum out on another adventure.

'But I'm old,' she said, 'and tastes have changed, and that's why you may not see as many Mina Todhunters about as when you were young. But when things were at their best I had a very good run for my money. I've had a good life and am grateful to all my readers for what they've done for me.'

She sat down and was greeted by enthusiastic applause.

Peter was the next to be introduced by Edward Clarke and to stand up and address the audience.

His tone was facetious. He claimed that he had taken to writing science fiction because science itself was utterly beyond him. The only way in which he could approach it was to invent it. Reading the works of other writers of science fiction had helped him a great deal. He had never actually copied them, but had found their fantasies stimulating. The worst mistake that he had ever made was to become intimate with some genuine scientists, physicists, chemists, biologists, even though some of them assured him that they enjoyed his works. He simply did not believe them and they made him feel a fool. But the books sold very well and he enjoyed writing them all. What more could he ask? He laid no claim to their literary quality and thought that he was very fortunate to be able to give people what they wanted.

He sat down and again there was applause, not as enthusiastic as that which had been given to Mina Todhunter, who after all was a well-known local figure, but sufficient to make him feel that he had played his part adequately. After him Simon Amory was introduced, stood up and was immediately greeted with applause before he had begun to speak.

Andrew felt that he was at a disadvantage, listening to Amory. Not having read the book, *Death Come Quickly*, nor seen the play or the film that had been based on it, and having by now acquired the feeling that Simon Amory was really a very difficult person to know, he discovered in himself a curious antagonism to the man which did not please him. For it must be founded, he thought, as Peter thought of himself, on jealousy. Simply jealousy of success, a most contemptible emotion. It could not have anything to do with a feeling about the man's work, for even the television version of it that he had seen had been interrupted by the telephone ringing in the middle of it, and Andrew switching off the set and talking on the telephone for several minutes. When he returned to the screen a great many things seemed to have happened, which was very confusing. There appeared to have been a murder, some incest had been discovered, some blackmail was being threatened, and there was some unexpectedly subtle comedy. Yet it was all in a strangely low key so that it was impossible to think of it as a thriller or a crime story or whatever such things were called nowadays. Was it possible that it was actually literature, Andrew had wondered, and had planned to buy the book. He had forgotten about this, however, and now felt embarrassed and annoyed with himself because of it.

Amory spoke only for a short time and said very little about himself. He spoke of the writers who had influenced him, Kafka, for instance, and Conrad and strangely enough, the great Victorians, but he said that he had not been aware of this until after his book was finished. He had never tried his hand at writing when he was young, he said. He believed he had not had the courage. To write seriously, he said, required great courage and he had not found this in himself until he was living alone with no one close to him who might be hurt by what he wrote. Andrew found that a little pretentious, but then began to wonder if he was being unfair, because perhaps the book was really as good as people said, which would entitle Amory to take himself seriously.

He sat down to a roar of applause.

'And that's that,' Rachel said in Andrew's ear. 'I wonder how many of them have actually read the book? Now come the questions.'

The first question, which was shot at Amory, was after all not as to whether he wrote by hand or on to a typewriter. That was the third question. The first was from someone who wanted to know where his ideas came from. It was meant for Amory to answer, but was neatly fielded by Mina, who used one of her hearty laughs to prevent his having to answer, then she went on to say that she had never known where her ideas came from apart from out of her head, and as the questions continued she took it on herself to answer most of them, to which neither Amory nor Peter seemed to have any objection. Amory had been very nearly correct when he had spoken during dinner of the questions that they were sure to be asked. He soon began to look very bored, though Peter kept up a better show of being interested. After a little while something made Andrew look round to see how Magda Braile and Desmond Nicholl appeared to be enjoying themselves. He saw then that they had gone. The seats that they had taken at the beginning of the performance were empty.

They did not reappear in the bar when most of the audience drifted there for coffee when the questioning began to die down and Edward Clarke decided to give a vote of thanks to the performers and to indicate that the show was over. Peter joined Andrew and Rachel as they made their way to the bar, but almost at once someone thrust a copy of one of his books at Peter and asked him to sign it. Other people were doing the same to Amory, but no one seemed to have any book for Mina Todhunter to autograph. Andrew wondered if she minded. If she did, she did not show it, but settled down at a table with an old woman who was obviously a friend and started what appeared to be a low-voiced intimate chat. Peter struggled to the bar to obtain coffee for Rachel and Andrew, but by the time that he had succeeded in bringing it to them Rachel had moved away and disappeared among the crowd. Peter kept the cup that he had brought for her for himself.

'Well, are you sorry you came?' he asked Andrew. 'Was it awful?'

'As if I'd say, even if it was,' Andrew replied. 'But as a matter of fact, I enjoyed it very much.'

'Are we going to meet sometime tomorrow?'

'Doesn't that depend on your host? He may have plans for you.'

'No, he's made it quite plain that he means to stick to his usual routine, working in the morning, and hoping not to be troubled by me before lunch. So if it should be a nice day and you feel like a walk, we might meet and get out on to the cliffs.'

'I like the idea, but you'd better phone me in the morning to confirm it.'

'I'll do that. Meanwhile, we've got to arrange how we're going to get you back to your hotel now. I assume Simon will take you, unless he hands you over to Clarke.'

'It wouldn't be far to walk, would it?'

Peter considered it. 'Not really, but it seems a bit snobbish to insist on walking when you've the chance of a drive in a Rolls. Let's get hold of Simon now and find out what his plans are.'

They had made their way through the crowd to where Amory was standing, the centre of a little group of admirers, and for the time being it was hardly possible to discuss the question of how Andrew was to return to the Dolphin.

Presently, however, the crowd began to thin and Amory turned to Andrew.

'Can I drive you back to your hotel?' he offered. 'I think we could decently leave now.'

'That's very kind of you.' Andrew replied. 'Thank you, I'd be grateful for it.'

'We must round up Rachel,' Amory said. 'Where is she?'

Peter looked round, shook his head and said, 'Gone to the loo.'

She was certainly not in the bar.

Mina Todhunter came up to the group, then put an arm round Amory's shoulders and said, 'Poor Simon, I believe you suffered horribly this evening, but you did very well. I'm off now. What about tomorrow? Same as usual?'

'Yes, why not?' Amory said.

'I thought as you'd guests you might want to change things.'

'If it seems desirable, I'll phone you.'

'Well, good night. Good night, Professor.' She shook hands heartily with Andrew and made for the door.

'We ought to have got her to take a look into the ladies' loo to see if Rachel's there,' Peter said. 'As a matter of fact, I haven't noticed her anywhere around for some time.'

'Perhaps she isn't well,' Amory said. 'I'll get one of the girls to take a look inside to see if she's there.'

He spoke to one of the young women who had been dispensing the coffee. She went out and returned in a minute or two, saying that there was no one in the ladies' lavatory.

'Where is she then?' Amory said, looking round the room once more.

'Perhaps she's waiting in the car,' Peter suggested.

'It's locked and I've got the key,' Amory said.

'Then she must have taken it into her head to walk home,' Peter said. 'Andrew was only saying a little while ago that it isn't far.'

'If she was going to do that, she might have told us,' Amory said. 'However, I suppose you're right, and there's no point in waiting for her here. Let's go, shall we?'

The three men made their way out to the Rolls. They saw Edward Clarke getting into his Vauxhall and waved good night to him. The drive down to the Dolphin took only a few minutes. Andrew thanked Amory for his evening's entertainment and as he drove off, went into the hotel, acquired his room-key and went up to his room.

He was surprisingly tired. The day that had been intended as the beginning of a rest had turned out quite demanding. But tomorrow, he thought, in spite of perhaps going for a walk on the cliffs with Peter, which he would enjoy, he would be careful to take it quietly. He thought that he would look in at Mina Todhunter's bookshop and buy a copy of *Death Come Quickly*, and spend as much of the afternoon as he did not spend asleep in reading it.

But then he remembered that in the evening there would be a performance of *The Duchess of Malfi*. Peter would almost certainly drag him off to see it. If that woman whom he had seen briefly in the greenroom at the Pegasus Theatre, infuriating Amory, had actually more talent than he would have guessed from her performance there, it might give him a great deal of pleasure to see it. While he undressed he tried to remember some lines from it, but to his intense annoyance found himself only muttering:

> *'Among them was a bishop who*
> *Had lately been appointed to*
> *The balmy isle of Rum-ti-Foo*
> *And Peter was his name . . .'*

He could not clear his mind of this until he had been in bed for a while and sleep overcame it.

CHAPTER 3

Next morning Andrew had his breakfast brought to his room. He had coffee and toast and marmalade, then he cut a slice of the cheese that he had bought the day before and when he had eaten it had a shower, shaved and dressed.

It was half past nine by then and a fine morning. The sky was cloudless, and the sea, as he could see from his window, was calm and glistening. He did not think much about the evening before, except that he resolved that sometime later in the day he would go into Mina Todhunter's bookshop and buy a copy of *Death Come Quickly*. But first he thought that even if Peter did not telephone, as he had promised, he would go for a brisk walk along the esplanade, across the bridge over the little estuary of the Gall and up on to the cliff beyond it. He had slept very well and although the bishop of Rum-ti-Foo was still bothering him, he felt refreshed and pleased to be on holiday. When he considered it, he thought that in its way the evening yesterday had been quite entertaining. He was glad that he had been to hear Peter speak.

Before he had got as far as making up his mind to set out for his walk, the telephone rang and it was Peter.

'How are things?' he asked. 'The evening wasn't too much for you?'

'Well, I must confess the wild excitement of it was a bit of a strain,' Andrew replied, 'but I feel reasonably recovered.'

'No, I mean really,' Peter said. 'It kept you out pretty late.'

'Peter, just how old do you think I am?' Andrew asked. 'I'm not yet eighty. I hope I've still several years of such dissipation ahead of me.'

'That's fine then,' Peter said. 'How would you feel about a walk?'

'I was just thinking of setting out for one. It's a beautiful morning.'

'Suppose I join you?'

'That would be very pleasant. But are you sure your host doesn't want some of your company?'

'Oh, he's busy working. I'm free to do as I like. To tell you the truth, Andrew, I think he wishes I could find a good excuse for leaving to go home. He thoughtlessly invited me down here for the weekend, and now that our performance is over, he doesn't know what to do with me, except, of course, that we're going to *The Duchess of Malfi* this evening, or that's what I thought the plan was yesterday, but now it seems a little uncertain. Anyway, shall we go for a walk?'

'Delighted,' Andrew said. 'Are you coming to pick me up here?'

'I'll be along in a few minutes.'

Andrew put the telephone down and attended to putting on his shoes. If Simon Amory no longer wanted to go to *The Duchess of Malfi* the reason, he thought, was fairly obvious. Amory and Magda Braile had certainly once been lovers, but had parted with venom on both sides. She had done her best the evening before to enrage him, and he had reacted with the bitter anger that she had tried to evoke. Andrew found it very difficult to imagine the woman who had made that scene with Amory in the part of the Duchess. Was she enough of an actress to assume the tragic dignity that the role required? Or was it yesterday that she had been acting? In any case, Andrew thought, he would probably go to the play that evening.

He was waiting in the lounge downstairs when Peter arrived in his Mercedes. He was looking bright and cheerful and like Andrew, claimed to have slept well. They set off down the short roadway that took them on to the esplanade. The people who strolled along it, sat in the little shelters along the way, or in some cases were pushed along in wheelchairs, were nearly all elderly, taking their holidays in the pleasant quiet when the pressure of the season was over. The little waves, breaking on the beach, made a soft slurring sound as they spread coils of surf over the pebbles. There was the wonderful freshness in the air that comes only close to the sea.

Andrew and Peter walked the length of the esplanade, reaching the bridge that crossed the little river at the end of it, and began to climb the cliff that rose beyond it. Andrew was inclined to take it slowly, while Peter, without thinking, was soon some way ahead of him. Then he stood still and waited for Andrew to catch up with him.

'I haven't told you,' he said, as Andrew, a little out of breath, reached the point where he was waiting, 'something a bit odd happened last night. I don't know what to think of it.'

'That reminds me,' Andrew said, 'did you find that young woman there when you got home?'

'That's what I was going to tell you about,' Peter said as they continued up the cliff side. 'We got back to Amory's place without any sign of her, then Amory dropped me off at the front door and drove the car on to the garage. You know, that sort of wing that sticks out from the side of the house that looks like stables. I suppose it was stables once, but now it's garages. Well, he drove off to them, and as soon as he did so, that woman, Rachel Rayne, came out of the little summerhouse in the garden. Did you notice it yesterday?'

'Vaguely,' Andrew said. 'It's in a clump of hollies, isn't it?'

'That's right. It's where Amory works. It's really a very pleasant little place, made all of wood, with just a desk and a chair in it and a bookcase and a sofa on which I suppose he can go to sleep when inspiration fails. And there's a rather handsome rug on the floor, which I suppose is Persian, though I don't know much about that sort of thing. Amory was in there when I came out this morning. I gathered the rule is that when he's in there no one must disturb him. Anyway, yesterday evening, as I was waiting for him to come back from the garage and let me into the house, Rachel suddenly came out of the summer-house and ran, really ran, as fast as she could, as if something terribly important depended on it, to the back of the house, where there's a door into the garden. It was obvious she didn't want to be seen. There was no light on in the summerhouse, though I'd a feeling that there had been when we first turned in at the gate. And when Amory and I got into the house she was sitting in one of the easy chairs in the drawing-room, looking as if she'd been waiting there for us patiently for a good while. So what had she been up to, do you think?'

'Did you tell her you'd seen her?' Andrew asked.

'Of course not. I didn't want to get involved in whatever she might have been doing.'

'And you haven't told Amory either about seeing her?'

'No.'

'What did she say about having disappeared from the Pegasus without telling anyone she wanted to walk home?'

'Oh, she apologized. Said she was halfway home before it occurred to her she ought to have told Amory what she was going to do, but anyway he was so surrounded by people she probably couldn't have got through to him. And she decided on getting away and walking home

46

because crowds always got on her nerves and she'd the beginning of a headache. An awfully unconvincing headache, it seemed to me. But as I said, what do you think she was up to?'

They were near the top of the cliff where the ground levelled off and a path ran near to the edge of it. The sea looked a long way below them.

'Except that she wanted to have a good look round Amory's study when he was safely out of the way, I've no idea,' Andrew said. 'We can't tell if she was looking for something special or just wanting to take a look at how genius organizes itself. It just might have something to do with her sister.'

'But she's been dead for years,' Peter said.

'Yes, but the sort of thing I was thinking of . . .' Andrew hesitated. 'Well, suppose Rachel thought her sister had given Amory something which she felt really belonged to her, and she wanted to get hold of it. No, don't take any notice of that. I'm just saying the first thing that's come into my head. Almost certainly totally wrong. But that reminds me, I was thinking last night I really must get hold of a copy of this book of Amory's.'

There was a thoughtful, faraway look on Peter's face.

'D'you think she could have stolen something from Amory's desk?' he asked. 'Some paper, possibly, or even some oddment of jewellery that had come to her sister perhaps from their mother and which, as you said, she felt belonged to her. She didn't *look* as if she'd stolen anything when we found her in the house. I mean, she didn't look excited, or furtive, or scared, or anything.' He paused. 'Do you think I ought to tell Amory about having seen her come out of the summerhouse?'

'That's up to you,' Andrew said, 'but I'd be inclined to stick to your first feeling that you didn't want to get involved. It isn't as if you know Amory particularly well, or owe him anything. Now, about this book, d'you think I can get it at Todhunter's?'

'Oh, certainly,' Peter said. 'Her window was full of copies yesterday, wasn't it?'

'So it was. Well, I'll go there when we get back and pick one up. It looks to me as if I've been missing something.'

'Yes, it's good, it really is. It makes me feel I'd like to get to know Amory better, but it isn't easy. I have this funny feeling that he doesn't like me, so why did he invite me down? Perhaps the fact is that he doesn't much like anyone. Yet the book doesn't give you that feeling at all. It's pretty grim in parts, but at the same time there's a sort of – well, you could almost call it tenderness in it. I'll be interested to know what you think of it when you've read it.'

They walked on for some time and when they reached a point where the cliff path began to drop, leading down to a small cove that nestled in a curve of the cliffs, they turned back and presently, after descending the slope that they had climbed some time before, made their way to the shopping mall and Mina Todhunter's shop.

If she was at home, she did not appear. A younger woman served them, telling them that it was surprising how many people had been into the shop that morning to buy Simon Amory's book. She said she supposed that it was because of the show the evening before, then looking at Peter with sudden surprise, asked him if he had not been one of the writers on the platform. He admitted that he had been, and she then assured him that she believed she had read everything that he had ever written. He tried not to look as pleased as he certainly felt, and when she thrust a copy of one of his books at him and asked him eagerly to autograph it for her, he did it casually, as if it were something that he was doing every day.

'Were you at the Pegasus last night?' he asked as he handed it back to her.

'Oh yes, I'm a regular member of the Literary Society,' she said. 'I wouldn't miss anything they put on. I'm going to *The Duchess of Malfi* too, tonight. I'm so looking forward to it. Really, the festival's been a great success.'

Andrew had been roaming round the shop, looking at what they had in stock.

'Miss Todhunter's had quite a revival, hasn't she?' he said. 'I'd very nearly forgotten her myself.'

Peter laughed. 'She doesn't write for people like you, I imagine. And now that I'm grown up you've no need to read her.'

'Well, naturally we always have a supply of her works here,' the young woman said, 'and during the holiday season, when people come here with their children, we sell quite a lot. And it isn't like the old days. If only they'd put some of her stories on television, I'm sure they'd have been a great success and probably be very popular still. But of course she's practically given up writing. She says she's too old and doesn't understand what young things want nowadays. I try to persuade her that's nonsense and that she could be as successful as ever if she'd only try, but she only laughs. She says why should she keep on working hard when she's got plenty of money. She only keeps the shop going because it's an interest for her.'

A door behind the counter opened just then and Rachel Rayne came out. She was in a dark brown trouser-suit with a brightly coloured scarf round her neck and had a shoulder bag slung from one shoulder. She looked startled to see Andrew and Peter there, and for a moment seemed uncertain as to whether or not she was glad to encounter them, then decided to give them a pleasant smile and to say that it was interesting to see how publicity really worked.

'I'm told they've had one of their busiest mornings for years,' she said. 'I see you've been buying Simon's book, Professor.'

Peter replied for Andrew. 'Yes, I don't think he liked the feeling of being one of the very few people who hadn't read it. Now what about a coffee, Rachel? I've discovered there's quite a nice place just round the corner from here.'

'That's a good idea,' she said. 'Thank you.'

'Andrew?' Peter said.

Andrew hesitated, uncertain as to whether his company would really be welcome to the two younger people, but Peter took hold of him by the elbow and said, 'Oh, come on. You've nothing else to do. Let's go.'

So Andrew walked along with Peter and Rachel to the coffee shop that Peter had discovered at some time since his arrival in Gallmouth, a small place with a row of tables covered in shiny plastic, and a counter with a coffee machine on it and plates of Danish pastries. Peter gave the order for the coffee and the three of them sat down at one of the tables. Rachel seemed to be in a thoughtful mood and did not respond to Peter's chatter about the evening before. Andrew wondered if she had any suspicion that Peter had seen her emerging from the summer-house and diving into the house by the garden door.

Suddenly she said, 'Professor, could I ask you for some advice?'

'Oh Lord,' he said, 'if there's a thing I don't like doing, it's giving advice.'

'But I've got to talk to someone,' she said. 'I thought I'd try Mina, but she just gave me a brush-off. I'm so bloody ignorant about such a lot of things, that's the trouble. In the old days I nearly always asked my sister what to do when I was in a muddle, she was so practical. You'd never have thought it to look at her, she seemed such a vague, gentle person, but she was really extraordinarily wide awake and sensible.'

'Yet she died intestate, didn't she?' Peter said. 'That doesn't sound very practical.'

She gave a start, staring at him with wide, bewildered eyes.

'Intestate?' she said. 'What on earth makes you think so?'

'Something Clarke said yesterday evening in the bar, after you'd vanished in the crowd,' Peter replied. 'Didn't you know it?'

She did not answer at once, then she said, 'No, I didn't.'

'Well, since I gathered she'd nothing much to leave, I don't suppose it made much difference,' Peter said. 'And in any case, I suppose she'd have left what she had to Simon.'

'Intestate,' she said, as if she were experimenting with the word. 'Intestate – really? What was it Edward Clarke said?'

'Oh, we'd got talking somehow about making wills,' Peter said. 'There's something about it in the book Simon's writing now, and Clarke said he'd come to him to find out from him, being a solicitor, how it really worked. Then Clarke said Simon really ought to know more about it than he did, because his wife died intestate.'

Rachel was still staring at him, her gaze intent.

'You're sure of this, are you, Peter?' she said in a curiously excited way.

'I'm sure of what Clarke told me last night,' Peter said.

'She died intestate,' she muttered, as if she were still trying to come to terms with the word. 'And I didn't know.'

'But would it have made much difference to you?' Peter asked. 'Wasn't it true that she'd nothing much to leave?'

'Oh, yes, absolutely true,' she said. 'A few thousand, left to her by an aunt, and that, as you said, naturally went to Simon. But if it had been more . . .' She gave a strange little laugh. 'I'm sorry, it's taken me so by surprise.'

'D'you think, if she'd made a will, she'd have left those

51

few thousand to you?' Peter asked. 'D'you feel Simon ought to have done something about it?'

'Oh no, no, why should he?' She picked up her shoulder bag, which she had put down on the table. 'You'll forgive me if I don't stay, won't you? I've just thought of something I ought to be doing.'

She got up and hurried out, leaving her coffee undrunk.

'Now what do you make of that?' Peter asked, staring after her.

'Perhaps the truth is that her sister had a lot to leave,' Andrew said, 'and she's got some idea that she can get some of it out of Simon.'

'But he only got rich after he started writing,' Peter said.

'And the little I know about intestacy,' Andrew said, 'which I picked up when a friend of mine died and I had to help to sort things out, is that the first two hundred thousand or thereabouts goes automatically to the spouse, and anything over that gets divided equally among the children, and if there isn't a spouse and there aren't any children, then it gets divided equally among the several relatives.'

'But how does that affect Rachel?' Peter demanded. 'Why should she get excited about it?'

'I can think of only one possibility,' Andrew said, 'though it wouldn't mean much unless Mrs Amory was actually a fairly rich woman.'

'What's that?'

'Simply that Simon Amory wasn't her spouse.'

'Not her spouse?'

'No.'

'But they'd been married for years.'

'Well, just suppose they weren't really, and Rachel knew it. And if that should be the case, she and not Simon would be her sister's heir. Doesn't it make sense of how she acted just now? And she may have dashed away to challenge him about it. For all we know a few thousands may mean quite a lot to her.'

'Andrew, what an imagination you've got!'

'Anyway, I'd prefer not to get involved in the matter, and if I were you, I'd keep out of it too. I don't see how either of us can help her.'

Presently they walked back to the Dolphin, where Peter had left his car and he drove off in it to Simon Amory's house while Andrew went into the hotel and into the bar, where he ordered a sherry. There was no one else in the bar at the time, but only a few minutes after Andrew had settled in a chair by the window Edward Clarke came in, accompanied by the two people of whom Andrew had had a glimpse the evening before, Magda Braile and Desmond Nicholl. Edward Clarke greeted him warmly.

'You're staying here?' he said. 'So are our friends whom you met yesterday. Of course you'll have lunch with us.' He bought drinks for the three of them and carried them over to the table at which Andrew was sitting. They sat down around it and Magda Braile gave Andrew a charming smile.

'We didn't really meet yesterday, did we?' she said. 'There was too much of a crowd in that room. But you're an old friend of Simon's, I presume.'

Andrew wondered how often he would have to deny this.

'As a matter of fact, I met him for the first time yesterday,' he said.

She raised her eyebrows. 'Really?' she said. 'I thought only old friends would have been allowed into that gathering. But come to think of it, perhaps old friends were just the people he wouldn't have wanted. I wasn't welcome, was I, and I'm a very old friend?'

Desmond Nicholl picked up the book that Andrew had

bought that morning, and which he had put down on the table before him.

'*Death Come Quickly*,' he observed. The skin stretched so tightly over his cadaverous face looked almost as if it might split if he ventured to smile. 'I wonder where he picked up that title. There are parts of the country where it's the name local people give to a small wild red geranium, though there are other people who call it Herb Robert.'

'All right, darling, we all know you're a botanist,' Magda said. 'But *Herb Robert* wouldn't have been much of a title for a book, would it?'

'Professor Basnett is a professor of botany,' Clarke told them.

'Are you really?' Magda said, as if this for some reason delighted her. 'And of course you knew where that title came from.'

'I'm afraid not,' Andrew said. 'I'm not that kind of bot-anist. You could take me for a walk in the most beautiful of woods and I'd hardly be able to name one of the wild flowers I saw there. My work was strictly in laboratories.'

'So you're not really a botanist, and you're not an old friend of Simon's, so what exactly are you?' she asked.

'I'm what's generally called a plant physiologist,' he answered, 'and I'm an uncle of Peter Dilly's.'

'Ah, so it was Peter Dilly you came to listen to – now I understand. What a charming little man he is. I'd like to meet him again. I enjoyed his talk much the most of the three. Do you think he'll be coming to *The Duchess of Malfi* this evening? And are you?'

'I don't know what Peter's plans are, but I shall cer-tainly be there.' Andrew had not made up his mind till just then that he would go to the theatre that evening, but he felt that it would have been discourteous to admit it. He was still finding it difficult, however, to imagine this woman in the sombre character of the Duchess. 'But it's only by chance I'm here. I didn't know, when I came to

Gallmouth, that there'd be a festival in progress, or that Peter would be on the spot.'

'What brought you then?' she asked. 'It seems a pretty dead and alive sort of place to me.'

'That happens to be what attracts me to it,' Andrew said. 'I've been coming here at intervals over several years. It's very restful.'

'Ah, I see,' she said. 'You come here when you want to get away from your hectic life in London. But you're retired, aren't you?'

'Yes.'

'Are you a Fellow of the Royal Society?'

'Yes, I am.'

'And you probably go to lots of their meetings and banquets and things, so you come to Gallmouth to recover.'

'Well, I shouldn't say that exactly describes my life in London,' Andrew said, 'but I sometimes get tired of my own cooking, so I thought a break in things before the winter begins to close in on us would be pleasant.'

'Ah, yes, the winter . . . D'you know, I really rather like the winter, though each time one comes round I say to myself, "How many more of these have you got?" I have a feeling I shall die in the winter.'

'You don't do anything of the sort,' Desmond Nicholl said in a quiet, cold voice. 'You don't think of dying at all. And why should you? You're a quite healthy specimen.'

'I tell you, never a day goes by without my thinking about it,' she protested. 'Being healthy has nothing to do with it. Life is so horribly dangerous. I could walk out of that door when we've had our lunch and be knocked down by a car and killed on the spot. Or our dear Simon could lose control of himself and stick a knife in my back, which is what he'd really like to do, you know. Didn't you see that last night? He hates me, he really hates me. And he's really very violent by nature, though he always keeps a tight hold on it. Poor Simon, I'm really so sorry for him. And I can't forget how much I loved him once. That's when I was a little girl. You know, Professor, I've known him since I was a child.'

'So really you've known him all your life?' Andrew said.

'Very nearly,' she replied. 'My father was vicar in Boringwood – that's a village in Hampshire I don't expect you've ever heard of – and Simon's father retired there after he came home from India. I'm not sure what he'd been doing there, but he became great friends with my father. But I didn't see much of Simon then. He was at Winchester, and only came home for the holidays. All the same, we made friends. He was really very good to me, and I worshipped him. He was so handsome and so good-natured. But he had a violent temper even then. Oh, my goodness, yes!' She gave a little laugh. 'We had a neighbour who had a son a couple of years older than Simon and much bigger, and if the two of them had the slightest excuse for it, they'd fight. And Simon nearly always came out on top, he was so much the cleverer of the two. And I used to love watching them battering each other, though I was dreadfully frightened too, but that was really all part of the enjoyment. And of course by the time I was about fifteen I was hopelessly in love with him. Did you know that children of that age can fall passionately in love, Professor?'

'I seem to remember having been through a phase of it myself,' Andrew answered. 'But I was rather faithless. I remember a girl for whom I thought I would be ready to die went down with measles, and by the time she came out of quarantine I'd attached myself to someone quite different.'

'All the same, you understand what I'm talking about,' she said. 'Desmond won't believe I was ever in love with Simon. He doesn't like to think I was in love with him during my adolescence, which I was, as I said – desperately. That's just jealousy, of course. He doesn't like to think I was really in love with anyone till I met him.'

'Oh, for God's sake!' Desmond Nicholl muttered in a tone of disgust. 'The trouble with you is that you've never been in love with anyone. Now, shall we go through to lunch?'

They finished their drinks and went through to the dining-room.

Edward Clarke was very silent throughout the meal, as indeed it was difficult not to be since Magda Braile kept up an incessant chatter. But he looked as if he had something on his mind.

In one of the pauses in the actress's talk, Andrew asked him, 'Are you worrying about the show this evening?'

'Somewhat, yes,' Clarke replied. 'A kind of stage fright perhaps. But everything's gone so well so far, I don't see why we shouldn't have a success with this too.'

'Oh, he's dead scared that I'm not the right person for the Duchess,' Magda said with a titter. She reached out a hand and laid it on one of Clarke's. 'You poor dear, you really needn't be frightened. When I get to work, I'm very disciplined. But talking of being frightened, I did scare Simon, didn't I? I didn't mean to in the least, but I could see it in his eyes when he first saw me, he was dead scared.'

'And how you enjoyed it,' Nicholl said sourly. 'But you needn't worry, Clarke. She'll pull herself together this evening. She tends to put on this sort of show before a performance. Nerves, I suppose. But sometimes she'll do the opposite and go dead silent. I'm not sure which is the harder to put up with.'

'How horrid you can be!' Magda exclaimed. 'I don't know why I put up with you.'

She went on with her chatter, mostly about Simon and how he had gone to Oxford and later broken her heart by falling in love with a woman whom he had insisted on marrying. She did not make it quite clear whether or not she had ever met the woman. Andrew found it a relief when coffee had been drunk and the party had broken up.

He went up to his room, intending to start reading the book that he had bought that morning, but making the mistake of lying down on his bed instead of sitting in his armchair, he was sound asleep in a few minutes. The sea and the unwonted exercise had made him very drowsy. He slept until nearly five o'clock when he was woken by the telephone ringing. Peter again, he presumed.

He was right, but he was startled by the tone of Peter's voice. It sounded high and excited, and he spoke very hurriedly, as if he were afraid of being caught at the telephone.

'Andrew, please come here as quickly as you can!' Peter said. 'At once! Please!'

'But why?' Andrew asked. 'What's happened?'

'I can't explain now,' Peter said. 'Someone else wants the telephone. But come –'

He stopped abruptly, and the dialling tone rang in Andrew's ears.

He put the telephone down and stood for a moment, looking at it in a perplexed way. He was quite ready to respond to Peter's anxious demand, but there were several matters to be solved before he could do so. First of all he had to discover Simon Amory's address. When Peter had driven him up to the house the evening before it had not occurred to him to mention its name or the name of the road where it stood. Now, if there was really a need for haste, the obvious thing would be to get a taxi, rather than to walk, though he remembered the distance as not very great. That the hotel people would certainly be able to solve for him. But first he must find the address. There was no telephone directory in his room, so he put a call through to the desk downstairs and asked them to find the address of Simon Amory.

They were slower about it than he had expected, but at last an answer came.

'I think Mr Amory's number is ex-directory,' a woman's voice said. 'I can't find it.'

This, after all, was not surprising, but for a moment Andrew felt completely baffled. Then he said, 'Oh, hold on a minute. Can you find the number of Miss Todhunter? She'll be able to give me the address I want.'

There was another pause, then the voice replied, 'Yes, here it is. Gallmouth 850415.'

'Will you put me through to that number then, please?'

In a moment he heard the ringing tone begin.

It rang six times before the telephone at the other end was lifted and a gruff voice said, 'Mina Todhunter speaking.'

'This is Andrew Basnett,' Andrew said. 'I'm sorry to trouble you, Miss Todhunter, but I need to get Simon Amory's address. It appears I'm wanted there rather urgently, and the fact is that although I was there for dinner yesterday evening, I didn't think of noticing the address. And it isn't in the telephone directory.'

'That's right, it isn't,' Mina Todhunter answered. 'He was always getting bothered by people wanting to interview him, or to get money from him for some cause or other, or just to meet him, so that he decided to be ex-directory. I believe it's helped. He's really a very retiring person, and he didn't like the incessant intrusion. But as a matter of fact, he's here now. Would you like to speak to him?'

Andrew felt that he had no desire to speak to Amory until he had spoken to Peter.

'Oh, I don't want to trouble him,' he said. 'But if you could just give me that address . . .'

'Yes, of course, it's Barnfield House, Cranleigh Road. If you're going by taxi, it'll only take you a few minutes. But please forgive my asking, is there something wrong that you're needed so urgently? I mean, your charming young nephew hasn't hurt himself, or anything?'

'I'm afraid I don't know,' Andrew answered. 'I don't think that's the trouble, because it was he who phoned me. But he did sound rather as if something was wrong. Thank you for giving me that address. I'm sorry to have troubled you.'

'A pleasure,' she said. 'I hope we may meet again. If you're staying on in Gallmouth for a little while perhaps you could find time to come in for a drink with me. Just call in when you're passing. You would be most welcome.'

Impatience began to grip Andrew. 'Thank you, thank you, I'll do that. Goodbye.'

He put the telephone down, hurriedly put on the shoes that he had kicked off when he lay down on the bed, went out and summoned the lift to take him downstairs. There he asked the woman on the reception desk to call a taxi for him, then he went to wait at the entrance door to the hotel.

As the minutes passed his impatience mounted, with growing anxiety that Peter would never have called him in the way he had unless something truly was wrong. Peter was a person who seemed never to worry unduly. He treated troubles which would have profoundly upset many people with casual acceptance. In his way, Andrew supposed, he had a good deal of courage. He could be casual because he was not afraid. Yet today it really sounded as if something had scared him.

It was actually a very short time before the taxi came, though to Andrew, waiting at the door, it seemed so long that he began to doubt if it was coming at all. Once he went indoors to the desk to ask the receptionist if she was sure that a taxi had been available when she called. She reassured him, and it was only a few minutes later that it arrived. Andrew gave the address of Barnfield House, Cranleigh Road, and wondered why the driver seemed to take so long compared with the drive in the Rolls the evening before.

But the taxi was not able to drive up to the gate of the house. It was stopped by a constable some yards before it reached the gates. There were police cars there in the road, and an ambulance and a number of men, some in uniform, some in plain clothes. Andrew leapt out of the taxi, and thrust his way forward to the gates. From there he could see that the centre of interest for all these people was the summerhouse among the holly trees. The door was open and although it was hardly dusk yet there was a light shining out of it. While he was standing there, with a cold sense of apprehension holding him rigid, he saw two men approach the door, carrying an empty stretcher.

CHAPTER 4

Andrew talked his way into the house. First a massive constable stopped him, then a sergeant. But the statement that he had been summoned by Peter Dilly acted like a password. The sergeant told him that the inspector would want to speak to him, but that meanwhile he could wait in the house. He went in and found Peter standing on the stairs, as if that was the place where he felt best able to keep out of the way of the men who were in the drawing-room and the dining-room and yet keep an eye on what was going on there.

As soon as Peter saw Andrew he came leaping down the stairs, grasped him by an elbow and pulled him towards them.

'Come up to my room,' he said in a tense whisper. 'I've been watching for you. I'm glad you got here.'

'But what's happened?' Andrew asked as he let himself be hurried upstairs, and then, more emphatically, 'Who is it?'

'Rachel,' Peter answered.

'Rachel? And it's murder?'

'It could hardly be anything else, could it, with all that lot down there?'

'She's dead?'

'Shot through the back of her head – and I found her. I was alone in the house. That's why I got hold of you. I didn't know where anyone was and I couldn't stand being alone here.'

Peter opened the door of one of the bedrooms on the

first floor and led the way into it. It was a small, charming room with white walls, like most of the rest of the house, grey wall-to-wall carpeting, a yellow and white cover on the bed and bright yellow curtains. A door opened out of it into a small bathroom. There was an armchair by the window into which Peter flung himself, then immediately stood up, leaving it for Andrew, throwing himself down on the bed, then jumping up again, drawing the curtains, then taking two or three rapid turns backwards and forwards in the room.

When Andrew sat down in the chair Peter came to stand in front of him.

'I didn't know what to do once I'd called the police,' he said. 'I knew I had to do that and they came pretty quickly, but then I thought of getting hold of you. You've had some experience of this sort of thing. You've helped the police before. There was that affair of the dinner where the man got poisoned with cyanide, and the time that QC got blown up by a bomb. I had a feeling the inspector had heard of you, anyway he let me telephone you and said he'd want to talk to you when you came. I expect he'll want to do that quite soon, so I'd better get on and tell you what's happened.'

'How is it you're alone in the house?' Andrew asked. 'Where are that couple – the cook and the manservant?'

'It's their afternoon off. They cleared up the lunch, then they went off to the cinema, and I don't know where Simon is. I'd been out on my own, exploring the town a little, since it was obvious he wanted to be left in peace and the strange thing is I actually saw Rachel only an hour or so before she was killed. I saw her come out of a house in one of those rather grand Regency crescents in the middle of the town. I was strolling along and I suddenly saw her come dashing out of one of them and go striding off in this direction. She didn't see me. But out of curiosity I went past the house she'd come out of and I saw a brass plate beside the door with the names Merridew Clarke Latham on it. Solicitors, I think.'

'Clarke,' Andrew said. 'You're sure of that?'

'Oh yes, because I thought just what you're thinking now, that she'd been to see that man Edward Clarke, and for some reason seeing him had got her into a pretty excited state. That was what she looked, at any rate. Well, I didn't come home immediately, but when I did I naturally expected to find her here, and when I didn't I assumed she was lying down in her room. Then I began to feel uneasy, not because of her, but because there was no sign of Simon. I'd realized he didn't worry at leaving his guests to look after themselves, then I began to get annoyed about it. I thought he went a bit far with it and that it was really bloody ill-mannered, so I thought I'd go out and interrupt genius at work in his summerhouse. Then a funny thing struck me. It wasn't dark yet, but you'd have expected anyone who was working in that place to have wanted a light. But there was no light in the window. So I thought the story of his wanting to work there was just a yarn and that he was probably sound asleep on his sofa. And I went out there and knocked and got no answer, so I opened the door and . . . and there she was, Andrew. It was a fearful shock. She was lying on the floor in the middle of the room, with what looked like the back of her head blown away, and there was a lot of blood . . .' Peter's voice began to shake. 'That's what they've told me had happened. She'd been shot at close range through the back of her head, so it couldn't have been suicide, it was murder. For one thing there was no gun there. The murderer took it away with him.'

'You've told all this to the police, have you?' Andrew said.

'Oh, yes, and a lot more, about what I'm doing here and so on. And I think I'm at the top of their list of suspects. Don't they say that if it isn't a family affair, when

64

the husband or the wife comes first, then the person who reports the finding of the body is the prime suspect. I'm very glad you're here, because talking to you is giving me back some sense of proportion. I've been feeling bloody scared, that's the truth.'

'I doubt if you need be,' Andrew said. 'There's a fact you haven't mentioned, that you met Rachel Rayne for the first time yesterday. That's true, isn't it, Peter?'

'Of course it is.'

'Well, that doesn't give you much time for working up a motive for killing her, unless, of course, you're one of those people who need to do a little killing from time to time just to keep themselves going. No, I shouldn't complicate things by imagining you're going to be suspected of murder. But I believe I know something that you don't. I know where Simon Amory is. He's with Mina Todhunter.'

'How do you know that?' Peter asked.

'When you telephoned me to come up here you omitted to give me the address of the house, and it isn't in the telephone directory, so I phoned Miss Todhunter, and asked her for it. And she mentioned that he was with her and asked me if I wanted to speak to him. I said I didn't want to trouble him and that the address was all I wanted, and that was that. Of course, I can't really swear that he was there, as I didn't speak to him, but if he wasn't she wouldn't have risked asking me if I wanted to speak to him, would she?'

'No. No, I see what you mean. So you don't think he's a suspect either.' Peter dropped down on to the bed again, giving a sigh, as if he felt that he had shed a load. He even managed to give a small smile. 'Yet he's the obvious person, isn't he? I mean, so far as we know, he's the only person with a relationship with Rachel that goes farther back than a week ago, when I believe she arrived.'

'We don't know that for certain, do we?' Andrew said.

'What was she doing, visiting Clarke this afternoon, if she didn't know him a bit better than appears. Incidentally, what was he doing in his office on a Saturday afternoon? I believe that's unusual for a solicitor. And what was she doing visiting Todhunter yesterday morning?'

'She said she'd gone to her for advice and had been given a brush-off.'

'Yes, and of course that needn't mean that she'd known her before she came here. She was asking me for advice only a little while later. And I gave her a brush-off too, about which I'm beginning to feel pretty bad. Perhaps if I'd listened to her, helped with her problem, whatever it was, this fearful thing wouldn't have happened.'

'Do you think it was for that advice that she went to Clarke?'

'It's what one usually goes to solicitors for.'

Peter stood up once more and again began to roam restlessly about the small room.

'D'you remember how excited she got when I said her sister had died intestate?' he said.

Andrew nodded.

'Well, suppose you were right,' Peter went on, 'and that the Amorys weren't really married, which would make Rachel her sister's heir. And suppose her sister had far more money than we know about, and she went to see Clarke to check up on what you told her about intestacy, mightn't that make her quite a menace to Amory?'

'Except that he's got lots of money of his own, so I don't see why he would grudge it her. Besides that, as I told you, he was with Mina Todhunter this afternoon.'

'Ah, but what time was that?' Peter asked quickly. 'If it was after I telephoned you, it was after five o'clock. And I think it was about three o'clock when I saw Rachel come out of Clarke's office. So there's something like two hours that Amory's got to account for. I believe he and Todhunter had a habit of playing chess on most Saturday afternoons, and she may be able to give him an alibi for all that time, but perhaps not.'

'I don't suppose they've told you anything about when they think the murder happened,' Andrew said.

'No, but I think the forensic people have got here by now,' Peter said. 'So they may know a little more about it themselves. I know fingerprint people and photographers and all that lot have got here. And I'm sorry to have hauled you into this, because now you're here, they may keep you.'

'I imagine they'd have hauled me in anyhow,' Andrew said. 'They'll be questioning all the people Rachel's been with since she got here. I wonder if this is going to affect the festival. Will they go ahead with *The Duchess of Malfi*, or will it be cancelled?'

'I don't see why it should be. None of the people Rachel's had anything to do with since she got here is involved in the play.'

'What about Clarke? Isn't he Chairman of the whole show?'

'Then I should expect him to make every effort to let things go ahead without any interruption.'

'Yes, I suppose you're right.'

The door opened. A constable looked into the room.

'Professor Basnett?' he said. 'Detective Inspector Mayhew would like to speak to you.'

Detective Inspector Mayhew was a tall, solidly built man with a heavy, square face in the middle of which the features seemed to occupy too little space. They were all small. His eyes were small, pale grey and close together above a short nose. His mouth was narrow-lipped and seemed to be gathered up into an expression of continuous distrust. His forehead was high, with the dark hair receding from it. His ears were surprisingly large and somewhat protuberant. Not at all a good-looking man, but with a certain impressive power about him.

He was seated at the long table in the dining-room. A much younger man was also seated at the table, with a collection of papers in front of him, on which he appeared to have been taking notes. A sergeant, Andrew guessed. The inspector waved Andrew to a chair, then gave him a long, steady look, as if he were memorizing him for use on some future occasion.

'I believe you're acquainted with a colleague of mine, Detective Inspector Roland,' he said. 'You were able to give him considerable help over the murder of Sir Lucas Dearden. I remember him speaking of you.'

'Sir Lucas Dearden – oh, a most unpleasant business,' Andrew said. 'And for me personally a tragedy. It lost me the friendship of two of my oldest and best friends.'

'I believe it was because you knew something of their background that you were able to help,' the inspector said. 'I'd like to know if there's anything you know of the background to this crime that could save us wasting a lot of time.'

'I'm sorry,' Andrew said. 'I'm a complete stranger here. I met Miss Rayne for the first time yesterday evening at a small dinner party given by Mr Amory. And I met Mr Amory for the first time then. I came down here simply to have a peaceful holiday. I've come here quite often over the years, and I always stay at the Dolphin, but I've no acquaintances in the town and I know nothing about the background of any of the people whom I met last night. I can tell you one thing, however, if you don't already know it. At this moment I believe Mr Amory is playing chess with Miss Mina Todhunter at her home. I've been given to understand that he does this every Saturday afternoon.'

The inspector gave a quick glance at the sergeant, who got up and went out of the room, presumably to telephone Miss Todhunter, or possibly to send a car to pick up Simon Amory.

'Thank you, Professor,' the inspector said, 'that may save us some trouble. But how did you come to know it?'

'I'd had a rather alarmist telephone call from my nephew,' Andrew said, 'asking me to come up here immediately, but he omitted to give me the address of the house. And when I looked for it in the directory, it turned out not to be there. Apparently Mr Amory keeps his number ex-directory. So I thought of telephoning Miss Todhunter, whom I'd met at that dinner party last night, and asking her to give me the address, which she did, and at the same time she mentioned that Mr Amory was there with her and asked me if I wanted to speak to him.'

'And did you speak to him?' Inspector Mayhew asked.

'No, I felt I wanted to speak to my nephew before I spoke to Mr Amory. My nephew had given me no hint of why he wanted me so urgently and for all I knew it might be for some reason that had nothing to do with Mr Amory. I may say, incidentally, that my nephew isn't normally an excitable character. He takes most things rather lightly, so I was sure from his tone that something was seriously wrong, though I wasn't prepared for anything as seriously wrong as it turned out to be. But I was anxious to speak to him before bringing anyone else into the trouble, whatever it was.'

The inspector took his lower lip in his fingers and gave it a little tug. The gesture had the effect of making him look exceedingly dubious.

'Can you tell me how you happened to be at that dinner party yesterday if you'd never met Mr Amory before?' he asked.

'As I suppose you know by now,' Andrew answered, 'my nephew's spending the weekend here. I didn't know it, and he didn't know I was coming, but we met by chance in the town in the afternoon. He told Mr Amory about it, and he invited me to the dinner, and to the show they were putting on in the Pegasus Theatre.'

'Ah, so you went to that.'

'I did.'

'Anything special strike you about it?'

Andrew was about to say no, nothing, when he remembered that of course two things had happened, of which one, at least, might be of importance now. He spoke of the first, however.

'Well, there was one odd incident just before the show began,' he said. 'We were in a greenroom under the stage, Mr Amory, Miss Todhunter, Mr Clarke, Miss Rayne, my nephew and I, when a man and a woman walked in and the woman threw her arms round Amory and kissed him, which appeared not to please him at all, but to infuriate him. And it was my impression that that was why she did it. He introduced her very reluctantly as Magda Braile, the actress who's performing this evening in *The Duchess of Malfi* in the Pegasus. I don't see what connection this incident can have with Miss Rayne's death, but you asked me if anything special struck me about the evening. Well, that was special in its way, I suppose. The intimacy and the antagonism between Amory and the woman – it isn't the sort of thing you often see.'

'Love affair gone wrong,' Mayhew observed. 'Was that how it struck you?'

'Pretty much.'

The sergeant returned to the room just then, gave the inspector a brief nod and sat down again at the table.

'Anything else strike you?' Mayhew asked.

'Yes, something that may be more important,' Andrew replied. 'When it was time to go home Amory was going to take Miss Rayne, my nephew and me in his car first to my hotel to drop me off, then on up here. But Miss Rayne had disappeared. We waited around for her for a little, then decided she'd probably decided to walk home on her own, and we set off. And what's interesting is simply something my nephew told me. When he and Amory got

70

back, Amory dropped my nephew off at the door and drove the car on to the garage. And while my nephew was waiting for him to return he suddenly saw Miss Rayne come running out of that summerhouse where you found her today and make a dash for the door at the back of the house, evidently very anxious not to be seen by Amory. But you'd better get the story direct from my nephew.'

'The summerhouse,' the inspector said thoughtfully, tugging at his lower lip. 'Yes, the summerhouse.'

'And the gun,' Andrew said. 'What about the gun?'

'Missing,' the inspector answered.

Peter was questioned after Andrew, but he could not yet have told Inspector Mayhew much when Simon Amory walked in. His thin, sharp-featured face was grim. He made it plain that he thought that it was he and not Peter who should be talking to the police, no doubt questioning them rather than being questioned, and the inspector seemed to accept this as reasonable. Peter was allowed to leave the dining-room and Amory went into it. The door was shut upon him, and Peter and Andrew went into the drawing-room, which happened at the time to be empty. From the window they could see the summerhouse and the people grouped around it and their busy coming and going. They could also hear people tramping about in a room overhead, probably Rachel's room, Andrew thought.

'I wonder how long they're going to keep me here,' he said. 'I'd like to get back to the hotel. If they let us go, will you come along and have dinner with me, Peter?'

'If Amory isn't expecting me to have dinner with him,' Peter said. 'I suppose I'll have to put that first. But the chances are he won't specially want my company.'

'It's occurred to me there's something I didn't tell the inspector,' Andrew said. 'I said nothing about Rachel's

71

curious reaction when you told her her sister had died intestate.'

'What do you make of that now yourself?' Peter asked.

'Nothing, really. I did have that idea that perhaps Lizbeth and Amory hadn't been really married, which would have made Rachel her heir, and that could have given Amory some sort of a motive for wanting to get rid of Rachel. But he's got enough money of his own not to need to grudge it her.'

'But what about blackmail?' Peter said.

'Blackmail?'

'Well, if Rachel knew they weren't married and threatened to make that public.'

'Nowadays?'

'You don't think that it would matter nowadays?'

'Well, would it?'

'I suppose not.'

'Not unless there are complications we don't know anything about, which I suppose isn't unlikely. But the poor woman's been dead for several years. I can't imagine how it could possibly matter to anyone if she and Amory weren't really married.'

'Suppose she'd left something behind that Amory couldn't afford to have made public, and Rachel knew about it, and was searching for it in the summerhouse.'

'Ah, now that's a much better idea.'

'There must be some reason why she went into the summerhouse yesterday evening, and then again this afternoon, once Amory was out of the way, playing chess. He was an accountant before he took to writing, wasn't he? Suppose he was involved in some important fraud.'

'I suppose it's possible.'

'Or it might be simply that he knows about the fraud and has been holding it over the head of whoever committed it. In fact, it's he who's a blackmailer. And Rachel believed he had some evidence which he kept in the summerhouse, and she was trying to find it to destroy it.'

'Why would she do that?'

'Well, if the person who's being blackmailed is a friend of hers, say. Or she was thinking of taking over the blackmail herself.'

'Oh dear, this is going too fast for me,' Andrew said.

'You don't think there's anything in what I'm suggesting,' Peter said, looking disappointed.

'Oh, there may be, there may be.'

'But you don't find it convincing.'

'I didn't say so.'

'But you don't, do you?'

Andrew had sat down in one of the easy chairs. He stretched his legs out and folded his hands behind his head.

'I think it's too early to start any theorizing,' he said. 'But if I were you, I'd offer all these ideas to the inspector. He's in a position to check them, which you and I are not. Now I do hope I can get back to the hotel fairly soon. I'm very tired.'

But Peter was still pursuing his own line of thought.

'Of course, it wouldn't explain why she got so excited about that intestacy.'

'No.'

'Oh, Andrew —!' Peter exclaimed explosively. 'You've got some idea about all this, I know you have, but you won't talk about it.'

'I haven't, I really haven't,' Andrew said. 'I believe in leaving things to the professionals.'

'That isn't what you've always done.'

'Only because I wasn't left any choice. But this time it's what I mean to do.'

At that moment a loud voice in the hall shouted, 'Simon! Simon!'

It was a voice that could have belonged to no one but Mina Todhunter.

Apparently receiving no reply, she opened the door of the drawing-room and looked in. Seeing Andrew and Peter there, she came in.

'Is Simon here?' she asked. She looked both anxious and indignant, as if it worried her that she had so far been left out of what was going on.

'He's with Inspector Mayhew at the moment,' Andrew answered, hauling himself to his feet. 'They're in the dining-room.'

'But there is something I must tell this man Mayhew,' she said. 'He ought to know it. In the dining-room, you say. I think I'll go in.'

'Unless it's something very, very urgent, I'd be inclined to wait till he is done with Amory,' Andrew said.

'Well, it's urgent, of course it's urgent, or I wouldn't have come,' she said, but she stood still in the middle of the room, running her fingers through her cropped grey hair with an air of perplexity. 'When they came for him, Simon didn't want me to come. He doesn't realize I'm much tougher than he is and besides that, I can help him. They'd get round to me sometime anyway, and it seems to me the sooner the better.'

'Well, don't let me stop you, if you think you ought to break in on them,' Andrew said.

She gave a sigh and sat down abruptly in one of the easy chairs.

'Oh, I suppose you're right, what I've got to say can wait,' she said. 'It's only that Simon's been with me nearly all the afternoon. If they're suspicious of him, and I suppose they have to be suspicious of all of us, I can give him a perfect alibi. But do you think they'll believe me?'

'Is there any reason why they shouldn't?' Andrew asked.

'Only that we're such very old friends that they might think I'd be ready to lie for him. As, of course, I would be. But I don't really know what's happened here. They came to the shop and said Simon was to come back here with them, because Rachel Rayne had been found murdered in his summerhouse. And that was really all they said. Looking back on it, it seems a bit odd, don't you think? I mean, that that was about all they said. But Simon went with them at once, and when I suggested going with him, he said there was no reason why I should get involved. That's just like him, you know, wanting to save me being troubled. But as soon as they'd gone, I realized I ought to have insisted on coming, because if they're going to suspect him, and they are, aren't they? — aren't they, Professor?'

'It's something they'll be thinking about,' Andrew admitted.

'Well, there you are. I can clear him with a few words. But I wish I knew more about what's happened. Can you tell me anything?'

'Peter can tell you more than I can,' Andrew said, sitting down again. 'Peter, tell Miss Todhunter how you came to discover Miss Rayne's body in the summerhouse.'

Peter looked very unwilling to talk about it, but once more he told the story of how it was that he had been alone in the house, and going looking for Simon Amory in the summerhouse, had found there the body of Rachel Rayne. Mina Todhunter sat very upright in her chair, with her hands clasped together on the handbag which was on her lap. Occasionally her lips moved, as if she were repeating to herself what Peter was saying. Her eyes looked very big and bright as she fixed them on him.

'Really, really, it's too terrible,' she said as he stopped. 'And to think that she came to see me only yesterday morning. And I wasn't as patient with her as I might have been. If only one could look ahead, how differently one would act. But it's no good regretting things now. I was impatient with her, and so she went off and for all I know, she went to meet her murderer.'

'Actually, she joined Peter and me and we went to have coffee at a little café round the corner,' Andrew said. 'But I've much the same feeling as you, Miss Todhunter. She asked me for advice, and I was very unwilling to give her any. It's a thing I don't like doing. But if I'd listened to what was troubling her, perhaps it might have saved her. Not very likely, but perhaps it might have made some difference. Would you consider telling me what she asked you about?'

'Oh, it was about the market for children's books – '

But that was as far as Miss Todhunter got, for at that moment the door of the dining-room was violently opened and Simon Amory strode across the passage into the drawing-room.

He went to the fireplace where the remains of a fire smouldered in the ancient grate. He stirred the ashes with a poker, then tossed two or three logs on to them. He did not look at anyone, but when a few sparks had risen round the logs he stood upright, gazing down at them, still holding the poker in his hand as if it were a weapon. His trim body looked taut with anger.

'Well, Simon, what's happened?' Mina Todhunter asked after a moment, her rough voice unusually gentle.

He dropped the poker with a clang on the hearth.

'How do I know what's happened?' he demanded, turning round to face the room. 'They've made up their minds I did it, that's all I can tell you.'

'But I can prove you didn't,' she said. 'You were with me nearly all the afternoon.'

'And you think they're going to believe that?' He directed his anger at her, as if she were to blame if the detectives did not believe her.

'I'll see that they do,' she answered calmly. 'But tell me, do they know what Rachel was doing in the summer-house? Was she looking for something? And is anything

76

missing? Did the murderer take anything? Have you been able to clear that up for them?'

'No, because they haven't allowed me to go in there yet. That's to say, I could tell them that one thing's missing, because they told me that the bottom drawer of my desk is empty, and there was only one thing I kept in that drawer.'

'Your manuscripts!' she exclaimed.

'My manuscripts!' he agreed.

'But, Simon, that's terrible!' She looked deeply concerned. 'They're valuable.'

He gave a small laugh of derision. 'Not as valuable as all that. Losing them doesn't break my heart. I only kept them out of a sort of sentimentality. But it's such nonsense. To kill a poor woman just to get your hands on two or three manuscripts that won't fetch anything once this craze for my stuff is over – because it's not going to last. I don't delude myself about that.'

'You say two or three manuscripts,' Andrew said. 'Had they all been published?'

'Yes, and that just proves what I was saying,' Amory said. 'I had my big bit of luck with *Death Come Quickly*, then I had two more books published, and they've attracted no interest at all, though in my opinion they're both of them better than that first one. It won't take long for me to be forgotten. So why steal those manuscripts?'

'Perhaps it was a lunatic who collects original manuscripts,' Peter suggested.

'You're damn right it was a lunatic –' Amory broke off as the door of the dining-room opened and Detective Inspector Mayhew and the sergeant came into the drawing-room.

'If you'd come down with me now, Mr Amory,' Mayhew said, 'and take a look round the summerhouse, I'd be grateful. You'll be able to say if anything's missing besides those manuscripts you mentioned.'

'Very well,' Amory moved towards the door. 'Though there's never been anything there of the least value.'

'But possibly someone thought there would be,' Andrew said. 'Did you never keep money there?'

'Never. I keep my money in the bank, except for what I need for day-to-day expenses, and that stays in my wallet.' Amory gave a slight slap to his hip pocket.

'Well, we'll go into that in more detail when Mr Amory has had a chance to look around,' Mayhew said. 'Shall we go, Mr Amory?'

'Inspector, just a moment,' Andrew said. 'I'd like to get back to my hotel, if you've no objection. I don't think I can be of any help to you here. You'll be able to find me there if you want me.'

'That's all right, Professor,' Mayhew said. 'There's no reason for you to stay here.'

'And I'll drive my uncle down to the Dolphin, if that's all right too,' Peter said. 'Then I'll come back here.'

Miss Todhunter rose to her feet.

'No one has thought of introducing us, Inspector,' she said, 'but my name is Mina Todhunter and I very much want to have a talk with you.'

'Certainly, Miss Todhunter – presently,' Mayhew said. 'I just want Mr Amory to take a look round the summer-house, then I'll be very grateful for anything you've got to tell me.'

Amory strode out of the room and the inspector and the sergeant followed him.

Peter prepared to follow them too, but Andrew, looking at Mina Todhunter, paused.

'Perhaps we should wait till they come back,' he said. 'I don't like the thought of leaving you alone in this empty house.'

'That's very kind of you,' she said, 'but you really needn't worry. I'm used to being alone. And the garden is still crawling with policemen.'

'That's true,' Andrew said. 'But if we don't leave at once, perhaps I could ask you something. You were interrupted when you'd just started to tell us what advice Miss Rayne came to ask you for this morning. You'd just said it was something to do with the market in children's books, but Amory came in then and you didn't finish. But perhaps that was really all it was. Is that so?'

'Well, yes, more or less,' she answered. 'It seems she wanted to make a bit of extra money by writing, and she'd thought of trying her hand at children's books. A great mistake, I told her. You've got to have a peculiar sort of mind to pull it off. Some people can do it and some can't. Knowing much about children has nothing to do with it. I advised her not to waste her time over it. I think she was a bit put out, anyway she left very abruptly. I said I was sorry I couldn't help, but after all, my own books don't sell much nowadays, so I'm hardly the right person to consult.'

'I see. Thank you,' Andrew said. 'Well, come along, Peter, if you're really going to run me down to the Dolphin. Good evening, Miss Todhunter.'

'Good evening, Professor. I hope we'll meet again.'

'I should think that's inevitable,' Andrew said, and set off for the front door with Peter following him.

Peter's car was in the garage. He led the way there. As Andrew had supposed on his first visit to the house, the garage was what had once been stables. They got into the car there and Peter drove out into the steep road by which he had brought Andrew up on the previous evening. A wind had risen and the tall beeches by the roadside tossed their heads against the cloudy darkness of the sky.

They were both silent until they had almost reached the hotel, then Peter said, 'I suppose she was lying?'

'Miss Todhunter? Probably,' Andrew said. 'But why do you think so?'

'Only because if Rachel had wanted advice on writing

for children, and the Todhunter gave her a brush-off, she'd hardly have turned to you for advice on a subject like that. You don't seem quite the appropriate person.'

'That's quite true, but suppose she hadn't absolutely made up her mind that she wanted to write for children. Suppose she was wondering about biography, and she'd somehow heard, though I don't know how, that I'd been dabbling in that, she might have thought of questioning me about it.'

'As a matter of fact, I told her about your book,' Peter said. 'When she heard you were coming to dinner yesterday, she wanted to know all about you. But I still think Todhunter was lying.'

'I'm inclined to agree with you, though I'm not sure why,' Andrew said. 'Perhaps it was because Rachel said she found writing even a paper a strain.' The car had reached the Dolphin and had stopped at the entrance. 'Feel like coming in for a drink?'

Peter said that he did, and when Andrew had got out of the car, drove it into the car park, then rejoined Andrew. They went together to the bar, which was empty just then. Both of them had double whiskies and settled down at a table by the window. The long, brightly patterned curtains had been drawn over it, shutting out the reflections on the darkness of the glass.

'But if she was lying,' Peter resumed, 'what advice did Rachel really go to her for?'

'I dare say we shall never know that,' Andrew answered.

'Oh, come on, you can make a guess, can't you?'

'Can you?'

'Well, no, but you're much cleverer at that sort of thing than I am.'

'I'm afraid I haven't the faintest idea,' Andrew said. 'I only have that guilty feeling that I ought to have let her ask me whatever it was she wanted to. It might have saved her, for instance, from going to that summerhouse in the afternoon. I've no reason for thinking that it would have, but it seems likely she wanted help of some sort and I might have been able to give it.'

'Did you tell the inspector about Rachel's visit to Todhunter in the morning?'

'No, it didn't occur to me.'

'I suppose we ought to tell him.'

'Yes, we probably ought to tell him anything we can think of about the woman.'

'Like her visit to Clarke in the afternoon. I suppose it was Clarke she went to see and not one of the other partners.'

'Of course, he may tell them about that himself.'

'But if he doesn't?'

Andrew drank some of his whisky. 'You're in a very suspicious mood this evening, Peter,' he said. 'It isn't like you.'

'I've never been mixed up in a murder before – really mixed up. I mean, possibly the prime suspect.'

'Yet perhaps she only went to Clarke for the advice that Miss Todhunter and I wouldn't give her.'

'I'd still like to know what it was.'

The door of the bar opened and someone came in. Andrew was sitting with his back towards the door and did not see who it was, but Peter looked up and made a little gesture of greeting. The newcomer came to their table. It was Desmond Nicholl.

'Hallo,' he said. 'Mind if I join you?'

'Please do,' Andrew said and Desmond Nicholl pulled up a chair and sat down at their table. His haggard face was looking even more drawn than usual. Like Andrew and Peter he was drinking whisky. 'Are you going to the theatre this evening?'

'Yes – yes. I suppose so – yes, of course.' Nicholl sounded confused and worried. 'Have to hurry, actually. That's to say, if Magda comes here. We won't have time for dinner, just a sandwich, perhaps. Or she may have gone straight to the theatre. I'd have expected her to let me know if that's what she was going to do, but I've been in all the afternoon and she hasn't telephoned. Disturbing, rather.'

'She's been out, has she?' Andrew asked.

'Yes, she went out in the afternoon for a walk. She likes to do that. She said she was going up on the cliffs. And I'd have expected her back an hour or more ago, so I can't help worrying. Stupid, probably. She's almost certainly gone straight to the theatre. Are you going to it, by the way?'

'Oh yes, certainly, wouldn't miss it for anything,' Andrew said, then suddenly pulled himself up. 'No, actually I'm not sure that I can. I've said I'll be here all the evening, if I'm wanted. How very annoying.'

'I think possibly Nicholl doesn't know what's happened,' Peter said. 'Do you?' he asked Nicholl. 'Do you know what's happened up at Barnfield House?'

Nicholl gave him a puzzled look and shook his head. 'No, has something happened?'

'I'm afraid so,' Andrew answered. 'Sometime this afternoon that sister-in-law of Amory's, Rachel Rayne, was shot in the summerhouse up there.'

'Shot!' Nicholl exclaimed. 'Not – you don't mean shot dead!'

'Yes, shot dead,' Andrew said.

'Suicide? Accident? Murder?'

'Murder.'

'Christ!' Nicholl's face looked even more skull-like than it usually did. 'What happened?'

'I don't think anything much is known about it yet,' Andrew said, 'except that my nephew found her dead body in the summerhouse this afternoon, called in the police, and they've questioned us both, then let us go. She had been shot in the head, but the gun, I understand, is missing, which makes suicide or accident even more unlikely than does the fact that she was shot in the back of the head. I know the fingerprint people and the photographers and some forensic people were busy up there, but we weren't told what, if anything, they'd found out. The murder certainly happened sometime between three and five o'clock, because she was seen in the town about three and my nephew discovered her body about five o'clock.'

Nicholl glanced at his watch, as if to make sure that the hours of three and five were registered upon it, then the sight of it made him exclaim, 'It's late – much too late for Magda to think of coming here. She must have gone straight to the theatre . . . I'm sorry, I can't help worrying, in spite of this awful thing you've just told me. Who had anything against that poor woman? Not Amory, surely?'

'There's no reason really to assume it was anyone in Gallmouth,' Peter said. 'None of us here know anything about her. It might be someone who'd followed her from London. Or even from America. We don't really know why she left America, do we?'

'That's the sort of thing the police will have to find out,' Andrew said.

'There's nothing we can do about it.'

'No, and if you don't mind, I think I'll just go and telephone the theatre,' Nicholl said. 'I'm sorry, but I can't help worrying. So if you'll excuse me for a moment, I'll just go and do that.'

He got up and went hurrying out.

'Not much concerned at murder,' Peter remarked.

'On the contrary, I thought very much concerned,' Andrew responded. 'Didn't you see his face?'

'It's the sort of face that makes you think of murder, even when he's being friendly,' Peter said, ' "Alas, poor Yorick . . . ?" He should sell his skull to a theatre.'

'That's a gruesome thought, but I know what you mean.'

A moment later Nicholl came running back. He picked up the glass that he had left half full and swallowed its remaining contents at a gulp.

'I must go,' he said. 'Something's gone wrong. I don't know what it is, but Magda isn't there.'

'Not at the theatre?' Andrew asked.

'No. And you're staying here, are you? You don't want to come with me.'

Andrew stood up.

'As a matter of fact, I was just changing my mind about that,' he said. 'I'll leave a message with the porter, so that the police can find me if they want us. But I don't think that's likely. We'd be glad to go with you.'

'But, Andrew —' Peter began, protestingly, then at something he saw in Andrew's face he stopped himself. 'Yes, of course,' he said. 'We'll be glad to go.'

CHAPTER 5

Andrew and Peter let Nicholl drive off ahead of them. On the way to the theatre both were silent. Andrew knew that Peter was uneasy, disturbed by his change of mind, but he did not try to explain it since he would have found some difficulty in doing so even to himself. A strong impulse had moved him and they were nearly at the theatre before he began to think that there was not much reason for what they were doing. Peter parked the car and they went in at the entrance together, Peter buying the tickets at the box office. The little theatre was almost full. Their seats were near the back of the auditorium and as they settled into them Andrew noticed that they were a few minutes late for the opening of the play. But it had not yet begun.

Ten minutes later it had still not begun and the audience was beginning to grow restive. On the whole they were being very patient, as if they recognized that in an entertainment of the kind for which they had come such a thing as punctuality was not to be expected. But the sound of coughing and of the shuffling of feet was increasing. Once or twice a voice was raised in protest, a demand that something should start happening. A quarter of an hour had gone by before Edward Clarke stepped out in front of the curtain and raised a hand for silence.

'Ladies and gentlemen,' he said, 'I have some very grave news for you. I'm afraid our performance this evening must be cancelled. Our leading lady, Magda Braile, has been taken ill. We had hoped, up to the last moment, that she would recover sufficiently to be able to take her part in our play, which as you know, is the central part, but unfortunately that is impossible. So we must ask you to forgive us and to go home. Your money will be refunded at the box office.'

A silence had settled on the audience. For a moment after Clarke had finished but still stood where he was, watching to see how his announcement would be taken, there was no movement. Then with a few mutters of resignation the little crowd began to move, filing out slowly past the box office, recovering their money there and drifting away along the lamp-lit street. Here and there someone tried to push his way out more hurriedly, but on the whole the departure from the theatre was quiet and entirely orderly. Andrew and Peter both stood up, waiting for their chance to leave. There was no sign of Desmond Nicholl in the audience. It seemed certain that he was behind the scenes with the disappointed actors and actresses.

'What do you suppose has really happened to her?' Peter asked.

Andrew shook his head. 'Who can say?'

'Do you think she's really ill?'

'It's possible.'

'I suppose she could have had an accident of some sort while she was out on her walk, and not been able to let Nicholl know where she was.'

'You're thinking of hospitals, are you?'

'Well, suppose she'd been knocked down by a car, or something like that?'

'As she herself thought possible, if you remember.'

'You don't sound very convinced.'

'Because at the moment we've no evidence at all as to what's happened to her.'

'I wonder if Clarke and the cast actually know.'

'I've a feeling they don't, but I could be quite wrong.'

They had begun to move towards the exit.

'I'll take you back to the Dolphin,' Peter said, 'then I suppose I'd better get back to Amory's place. I don't suppose the police expected me to be away for so long. I wonder if they've been looking for me.'

But when he and Andrew arrived back at the hotel they were told that no one had come looking for them. When he had made sure of this Peter returned to the car and drove off, while Andrew went back to the bar and ordered another whisky. After it, he went into the dining-room and ordered dinner. He had only just begun it when Nicholl came in.

As a matter of courtesy he came to Andrew's table and sat down facing him. He began to speak at once.

'She's still missing.'

'I'm very sorry,' Andrew said. 'Haven't you any idea what's happened to her?'

Like Peter, Nicholl said, 'She could have met with an accident. We've been on to the police about it, and we've been ringing all the hospitals. There are only three in the neighbourhood, and if she's been in an accident, it won't have been far away, as she was simply out walking. But none of them have any news of her. The police have taken particulars, but they seem to be much more involved in that murder up at Amory's than a mere missing person. God, Basnett, I'm worried! It's so unlike her.'

'She's normally very conscientious, is she?'

'Lord, yes! She'd never have let those people at the theatre down unless something really serious had happened. And an accident is the only thing I can think of. Some bastard knocked her down and left her lying there. Drove on and never thought of getting her to a hospital. Or she could have been taken ill, I suppose, had a heart attack or something, only she's physically as sound as a bell, or so we've always thought. And it isn't like her not to let me know what had happened to her, if she was capable of it. You may have got a wrong idea of her because of that scene she made with Amory. She did that just to annoy him.'

'They're old enemies, are they?' Andrew said.

A faint smile flitted across Nicholl's skull-like face.

'That's a word for it. Of course, they were lovers once, but that's years ago. I know hardly anything about it. I haven't wanted to know. We're married, you know, though she kept her own name for professional purposes. Not that it is her own name. That's Mary Baker. Yes, we're married. Have been for years, and it's been really good. Everything I ever dreamed of. And she's never let me down like this, so all I can think of is that she's been in an accident. Don't you think so yourself? Can you think of any other explanation?'

The flow of speech stopped for a moment, and Nicholl gazed at Andrew with eyebrows questioningly raised. He was talking feverishly, like someone who hardly knows what he is saying. Andrew felt that it was probably a very unusual thing for the man to do. He remembered Nicholl's total silence at the time of his wife's meeting with Amory. That was more characteristic of him, Andrew thought, than this desperate need to talk.

'I wish I could help,' Andrew said, 'but I think you're probably right.'

'Of course, it might not have been a car accident,' Nicholl hurried on. 'If she'd gone walking on the cliffs here, and slipped. I haven't been up on them myself, so I don't know how dangerous they are.'

'I was up on the cliff on the far side of the town only this morning,' Andrew said, 'and if she stuck to the path there I shouldn't say it was dangerous at all. On this side, as far as I can remember, there's a strip of beechwood between the road and the edge of the cliff. The wood doesn't go right to the edge, and the path beyond it is quite open and navigable.'

'No, no, I'm sure it was a car, only I can't think where it could have happened without someone having found her and reported it to the police or a hospital.' Nicholl looked at the food that had just been put down in front of him as if he could not think how it had got there. Like Andrew, he had ordered an omelette, but he did not look as if he intended to eat it. 'I never wanted to come on this expedition, you know,' he said. 'I thought it would be a waste of time. But Magda was very keen on it, and I'm inclined to think it was partly because she knew Amory was involved in this festival affair. I've a feeling she wanted to let him see just what she'd become as an actress. But I'm only guessing. We didn't talk about it. I think he was one of the bad things that happened to her in her life. In fact – you'll think this is ridiculous – I can't help wondering if he's had something to do with her disappearance. Balls, you'll say to me, and I know you're quite right. Only he did show his hatred of her yesterday evening, didn't he, and hatred like that sometimes has to express itself?'

He picked up a fork and jabbed at his omelette. Andrew had about finished his.

'Tell me what you really think,' Nicholl went on earnestly. 'Do you think Amory could have had anything to do with Magda's disappearance?'

'I believe Amory spent most of the afternoon with Miss Todhunter, playing chess,' Andrew replied. 'It's something they do every Saturday afternoon.'

'Even when he's got guests? He'd your nephew and Rachel Rayne. It hardly seems like the behaviour of a perfect host.'

'But it's apparently what he did.'

Nicholl managed to swallow a mouthful of his omelette, then pushed his plate away, muttering, 'I don't want this. I'll just have some coffee.' He looked round for the waiter and gave an order for coffee. As he did so a change came over him. He seemed to be stiffening himself, carefully erasing the expression from his face and gazing not at Andrew, but just past him at some spot on the wall. 'I hope you'll forgive me for burdening you with my worries,' he said in a flat, lifeless voice. 'Probably very embarrassing for you and all to no purpose. Not the sort of thing I usually do.'

'But entirely understandable in the circumstances,' Andrew said.

It was plain that Nicholl regretted having talked as he had, for he became quite silent and as soon as he had drunk his coffee said a terse good night to Andrew and left him.

Andrew had cheese and biscuits after his omelette. It irritated him very much that as soon as he was left to himself his mind became filled with the rhyme:

> *Among them was a bishop who*
> *Had lately been appointed to*
> *The balmy isle of Rum-ti-Foo . . .*

He knew that this afflicted him only because he did not know what else to think about, and that if only he could bring his mind to bear, say, on the problem of why and by whom Rachel Rayne had been murdered, or on the mystery of the disappearance of Magda Braile, he would be freed from this nonsensical way of occupying it. But the problems were too big for him to be able to grasp them and he was very tired. The habit of mumbling doggerel rhymes to himself was always at its most obsessive when he was tired. And there was no avoiding the fact that lately he had found himself getting tired far more quickly than only a year or two ago. He was getting forgetful about things too. Sometimes in the middle of a sentence he would find that he had forgotten what he had started out to say. When he had drunk his coffee he went up to his room.

Going up the stairs he made the rather satisfying discovery that the bishop of Rum-ti-Foo had been defeated by another quotation, and one with somewhat more dignity.

Cover her face, mine eyes dazzle. She died young.

It was not really surprising that he should find this filling his mind, since it was the most famous line in the play which he and Peter had failed to see that evening. But Rachel Rayne had not been so very young when she had died. Thirty-five at least. And Magda Braile, in the accident in which she had almost certainly been involved, if it had been fatal, had been somewhat older. Not that that would have been apparent when she was on the stage. What with make-up and skilful lighting, it would have been easy to make her appear young. But thinking about that in no way helped to explain either calamity. It did not even give a hint as to whether in some strange way the two incidents might be connected. There was no reason to suppose that they were, except that they had happened on the same day, and that probably meant nothing.

Andrew slept soundly that night, sheer fatigue overcoming him as soon as he got into bed. He had meant to start reading *Death Come Quickly*, but it remained unread on the table by his bed. In the morning he awoke in a puzzled state, feeling that something that he ought to know about had gone wrong. For a moment he could not think what it was. Then he remembered. Murder. Mysterious disappearance. Yes, certainly things had gone wrong the day before. His mind cleared, to find the maid trying to place his breakfast tray on his knees. Coffee, toast and marmalade, and then of course a slice of his own cheese. After that, shaving, a shower and getting dressed, and feeling more or less awake and normal by the time that his telephone rang.

He assumed that it was Peter calling him, but it was Detective Inspector Mayhew with a request that Andrew should meet him in the police station for a discussion of some odd things that had come up. Andrew arrived at the police station at about ten o'clock and was received by the inspector in his office, a small, clinically tidy room, in which he was sitting at a table on which some neat piles of papers were arranged. He rose to his feet when Andrew was shown in and shook his hand, then gestured to him to be seated in a chair that faced him across the table. His large, square face with the small features in the middle of it looked freshly shaved and considering that he had probably spent not very much of the night asleep, surprisingly alert.

With one of his small, tight-lipped smiles, he said, 'You understand, Professor, this is unofficial. If you can help me, I'll be grateful, but I realize you may be reluctant to answer one or two of the questions I want to ask you, and I'm not going to try to put pressure on you. It's your advice I want, as much as anything.'

'I hope then I can help,' Andrew replied.

'I want to ask you first,' Mayhew went on, 'whether to your knowledge, your nephew, Mr Dilly, had ever met Miss Rayne before this Friday.'

'To my knowledge, no,' Andrew said. 'Also, to the best of my belief, no. But I understand why you think I may be unwilling to answer your questions if they're all like that one.'

'Just so.' The distrustful little smile still puckered Mayhew's small mouth. 'But murder is a serious matter, even if one's nephew might be suspected. One might be ready to part with a little information concerning him. Sometimes even closer relatives will talk, parents about children, children about parents, husbands and wives about each other.'

'Are you telling me that you seriously suspect my nephew of this murder?' A hot little flame of anger stirred in Andrew's brain.

'No, no, only clearing the ground,' Mayhew answered. 'You're telling me that to the best of your knowledge and belief, Mr Dilly had never met Miss Rayne until the day before she met her death?'

'Certainly.'

'Can you tell me then what brought him as a guest to Mr Amory's house? I understand that his reason for coming to Gallmouth was to take part in the Arts Festival, but why is he staying with Mr Amory? They don't seem to be special friends.'

'All I know about that,' Andrew said, 'is that they met at a literary luncheon and Mr Amory suddenly invited him to take part in the festival, and to spend the weekend with him. Then the official invitation from the committee arrived a few days later and my nephew accepted it as well as Amory's to stay with him. But I agree the relationship doesn't seem to have ripened into friendship. My impression is that Amory is a somewhat difficult man. I imagine he gave the invitation on an impulse and has since regretted it.'

'For any specific reason?'

'For none that I know of. May I ask *you* a question now? Has anything been found out yet about the disappearance of Magda Braile?'

A small frown wrinkled the inspector's high, smooth forehead. It looked as if he disliked the question. 'Nothing yet,' he said.

'There's no trace of her?'

'The last that's been seen of her, according to our present knowledge, is when she left that hotel where you're staying, stopping for a moment to speak to the receptionist and say that she was going for a walk. Then she went off down the drive to the main road and vanished.'

'At what time was that?'

'About quarter past four.'

'You've no witnesses to where she went or what direction she took after that?'

'None have come forward yet.'

'She's after all a fairly well-known figure.'

'Perhaps not in Gallmouth. We're rather off the beaten track here.'

'Well, it's very disturbing.'

'Almost as disturbing as murder, one might say. Now, I wonder if you'd take a look at this.'

With a quick little gesture Mayhew tossed across the table to Andrew a small book with a cover of bright red plastic. Picking it up, Andrew saw the word, 'Addresses' printed on it in gold. He opened it and flicked the pages over. They were fairly full of names, addresses and telephone numbers, written in a small but sprawling hand. Then he suddenly put it down.

'Ought I to have handled it?' he asked.

'It's all right, it's been tested for fingerprints,' Mayhew said. 'There are a few very old and very smudged ones, and some of Mr Amory's. It was found in a drawer of the desk in the summerhouse. But it isn't Mr Amory's address book, it's his wife's. And I'd be grateful if you'd look through it carefully and tell me if anything special strikes you about it.'

Andrew considered it.

'You want me to do that now?' he said.

'If you would, but take your time,' Mayhew said. 'There's no hurry.'

Andrew began to turn the pages more carefully. He began at the beginning, wondering what he was supposed to find. None of the names there meant anything to him. He had reached the letter C and was reading the address and telephone number of Edward Clarke when a man came hurriedly into the room, bent down over Mayhew and muttered something into his ear. Whatever it was brought Mayhew immediately to his feet.

'Excuse me,' he said, already on his way to the door. 'Something important's come up.'

He left the room.

Andrew stayed where he was, continuing to turn the pages of the address book. After a time he took a small notebook out of his pocket and jotted down in it a name and address. Soon afterwards he closed the book, held it for a moment, looking at it thoughtfully, laid it down on the table, then he stood up and made his way out of the room and down the stairs to the entrance.

He spoke to the constable behind the counter there.

'Can you tell me the way to Linwood Drive?' he asked.

As he asked it the telephone on the counter began to ring, and at the same moment two men came hurrying down the stairs and out of the door to the street. Then another man came in at the door and went striding to a door that opened into a room in which there were already a number of men. The sound of a loud, clear voice reached Andrew, which seemed to him to be giving orders. As the constable put the telephone down, having answered it briefly, Andrew repeated his question.

'Can you tell me the way to Linwood Drive?'

The man looked at him as if he could not think what he was doing there, and found it difficult to bring his mind back from whatever it was that the telephone call had done to it. In fact, it was obvious that Andrew had chosen a very bad time for his question. Something of far greater importance was absorbing everybody. He had a chilly feeling that he knew what it was.

'Linwood Drive?' the constable said at last. 'Hm, yes, straight down till you reach the church, then turn left, then go on till you pass Marks and Spencer, then right, then cross the square and the road straight ahead of you is the one you want.'

'Is it far?' Andrew asked.

The man looked him up and down as if measuring what meaning the word might have for someone of Andrew's age. But he seemed reassured by what he saw, for he said, 'About ten minutes' walk.'

At that moment the telephone began to ring again, so Andrew only said a quiet, 'Thank you,' and went out into the street.

It took him rather more than ten minutes to reach Linwood Drive, for the directions that he had been given, though accurate, were hard to remember. Finding his way at last to the square, he found the street he wanted leading out of it. Walking along it slowly, he took his notebook out of his pocket and checked what he had written in it.

'C.W. Wale, 37 Linwood Drive. Tel 932875.'

The house for which he was looking was in a Victorian terrace of small houses, some of which had been rejuvenated with bright paint, and some of which looked as if they were quietly decaying. They had what had once been small front gardens, but most of which had been covered with gravel, with only an odd shrub or two appearing here and there. Number 37 had neither been brightened up with new paint nor entered yet into a state of decay. It looked neat and modestly unnoticeable.

Andrew crossed the little gravelled yard in front of it and rang the bell.

After a short pause he heard footsteps inside and the door was opened. A small woman who looked as if she was about fifty stood there, looking at him curiously before giving him a smile and saying, 'Yes?'

She was dressed in dark blue slacks and a bright blue and white striped sweater. Her grey hair was cut short, with a curly fringe falling forward over her forehead. Her eyes were a clear blue.

'Miss Wale?' Andrew asked.

'Mrs,' she answered.

'I'm sorry – Mrs Wale. There are a few questions I would like to ask you concerning Mrs Amory, if you can spare me a little time.'

She did not answer at once, but studied him thoughtfully.

'You *look* respectable,' she announced at length.

'Thank you,' Andrew said.

'And you're not police, you're over the age limit.'

'Indeed I am.'

'Then you'd better come in. Only – you aren't some kind of private detective, are you?'

Andrew hesitated for a moment, because although he was not by profession a detective of any kind, he was at the moment engaged in a sort of detective work. He avoided the question by asking another.

'Have the police been to see you, then?'

'Yes, only a little while ago,' she said. 'But come in. If you're going to ask as many questions as they did, we don't want to stay on the doorstep.'

She stood aside for him to enter, closing the door behind him, and took him into a small, cosy room with a bow window, neatly shrouded in net, overlooking the street, a flowered wallpaper, several comfortable chairs covered in bright cretonne, a desk with a typewriter on it, and what Andrew presumed was her dining-table, though there was only one chair drawn up to it. If a Mr Wale existed, it did not look as if he lived here.

'Well, get ahead with it,' she said when they were both seated on either side of the gas fire. 'What do you want to know?'

'You're a typist, aren't you?' Andrew said.

'You could call me that, yes.' She nodded her head. 'I don't do it regularly. I just take in the odd job from time to time.'

'Did you ever do any odd jobs for Mrs Amory?'

'*Mrs* Amory?' she asked.

'Yes.'

'The police wanted to know if I ever did any work for Mr Amory.'

'And did you?'

'No. But I did a couple of jobs for his wife before she died. I typed a couple of novels for her. But I don't think either of them ever got published. They weren't so very good, in my humble opinion. But she was a nice woman. I thought her death was awfully sad.'

'Was either of the novels you typed called *Death Come Quickly*?'

She gave him a puzzled look. 'That's a film.'

'But it started life as a novel. Did you type it for her?'

She shook her head. 'Definitely not.'

'Nor for Mr Amory?'

'I told you, I never did any work for him.'

'Do you remember how you got in touch with his wife?'

'I believe it was through Miss Todhunter. The lady who runs the bookshop. Yes, that's how it was. I've done one or two jobs for her. I believe she did a good deal of writing in the old days, but nowadays she seems to have given up. But when Mrs Amory took to writing and wanted a typist, Miss Todhunter recommended me. I can't remember how I first met Miss Todhunter. It was several years ago.' She pushed a hand through her curly hair, disarranging her fringe. 'Now will you tell me why you're asking these questions? Seems to me I've answered enough.'

'Thank you, you're being very helpful. Well, I was shown an address book this morning by the police which was said to have belonged to Mrs Amory, and it had your name in it, but not under W. It was under T. For typist, you see. And it struck me as curious, because to the best of my knowledge Mrs Amory had never done any writing. Her husband took to it after her death, and now of course

98

he's famous, but I've never heard any word of her trying her hand at it. As you've explained it to me, however, she did try, but without any success, and that's why your name is in her address book.'

'Looks like it,' she agreed.

'When she brought her manuscripts to you, were they just handwritten?'

'That's right, but quite easy to read, I was glad to find. Now will you tell me just what you've got to do with all this? I know there was a murder up at Amory's place, and I've had the police here, asking me just the questions you've been asking me now, but I don't know who you are or how you come into all this. Are you going to tell me?'

'My name's Basnett,' Andrew replied, 'and I came down to Gallmouth for a short change and a rest and I happened to run into a nephew of mine called Peter Dilly, also a writer, who's staying with Mr Amory for the moment. I'm staying at the Dolphin. And it was my nephew who discovered the dead body in the summerhouse, at a time when there was no one else in the house. So it's natural, I suppose, that he should come under a certain amount of suspicion, and so I'm doing what I can to solve a few of the problems connected with the case, to help to clear him.'

'You're certain then that he had nothing to do with the murder?'

'Quite certain.'

She gave him a quizzical look. 'Of course you would be. But what's the reason for worrying about my typing?'

'Only that several manuscripts, apparently by Mr Amory, which he kept in a drawer of his desk in the summerhouse, seem to have been removed by the murderer. Or by somebody. And when the police showed me an address book with your name in it entered under

"Typist", I thought you might be able to tell me a little about those manuscripts. As you have.'

'Well, I'm sure I'm very glad if I've been any help, but I don't see just how I have,' she said.

Andrew stood up. 'Oh, I think you have, and I'm very grateful.'

But the truth was that as Andrew walked back to the Dolphin he felt a good deal confused. He wanted very much to talk to Peter and resolved to telephone him to arrange a meeting as soon as he reached the hotel. But as soon as he did so he was intercepted by a white-faced receptionist who looked as if she would have liked to throw herself into his arms for protection from something or other, and who gasped out sharply, 'Oh, Professor Basnett, isn't it terrible? Nothing, *nothing*, like it has ever happened to us before!'

'Oh, I'm sure you're right,' he said. 'But just what's happened?'

'They haven't told you?'

'They?'

'The police. I thought you went to the police station this morning.'

So she was not above listening on the internal telephone system. Not that it mattered. It occurred to him too that the police had become 'they' to everyone who had had anything to do with them over the weekend, a curious abstraction, anonymous, faceless, hardly human.

'They didn't tell me much, they only asked me questions,' he said.

'So you don't know that they've found Miss Braile – or Mrs Nicholl, as I believe she's really called.'

'No.'

'At the foot of the cliff, not ten minutes' walk from here, her body mostly in the water, but she wasn't drowned. Her neck was broken.'

'That's indeed terrible.' Andrew remembered the chill

100

that he had felt in the police station when everyone had seemed suddenly to be propelled into urgent action, so that he was merely something in the way, and he recognized that it had been fear of some outcome such as this that he had sensed. 'Where's Mr Nicholl?'

'I think he's still at the police station,' the woman said. 'They came for him to tell him his wife's body had been found. Some children found it; isn't that dreadful? She'd fallen on to the rocks and was killed stone dead. It's a puzzle, because they say it must have been daylight when she fell, and the path there isn't dangerous.'

'It was from the cliff on this side of the town, was it, not the other side of the bridge?' Andrew asked.

He remembered the cliff path on the near cliff quite clearly from earlier visits to Gallmouth. It began almost opposite the entrance to the Dolphin and rose steeply, curving to the left where the strip of beech trees began and lying between them and the edge of the cliff, running parallel to the main road up which Peter had driven Andrew when they were on their way to Simon Amory's house.

'That's right,' the woman said. 'The children shouldn't have been playing where they were, it's not safe scrambling about on those rocks, but Mrs Nicholl can't have been doing that. She must have fallen over the edge of the cliff. I wonder if she was short-sighted and didn't like to wear spectacles because she thought they made her look old. A lot of people are like that.'

'Perhaps,' Andrew said. 'Perhaps. If anyone should want me, I'll be in my room. There's a telephone call I want to make.'

He turned towards the lift and summoned it from an upper floor, stepped into it and a moment later stepped out and went to his room. Picking up the telephone, he dialled Amory's number, of which he had made a note, and when he was answered by a man's voice belonging, he thought, to the man who had waited on the table at Amory's dinner party, said that he wanted to speak to Mr Dilly. He was told to wait a minute and after only a brief wait, Peter's voice said, 'Hallo.'

'Peter?' Andrew said. 'Can you come down here to lunch with me?'

'I'm not sure that I can,' Peter said. 'The place is swarming with policemen and I've a feeling I may be wanted. You've heard of the discovery of Magda Braile's body?'

'Yes, but it's about something quite different that I want to talk to you.'

'Can't you do it on the telephone?'

'No.'

'Well, I'll see what I can do. There may be no problem about it. But you see, when she was discovered there was that age-old question, did she fall or was she pushed? And it's probable that it happened, so I understand, around the same time, or not long after, Rachel Rayne was shot. Can't you give me some idea what it is you want to talk to me about?'

'About a case of fraud, as you yourself suggested. A fairly major fraud. It's complicated, however, and I may be quite wrong. But if I'm right it may explain a number of things that have been puzzling us. But I need to talk it over with someone. So come if you can.'

He put down the telephone, went out and summoned the lift once more, went down to the ground floor and on into the bar.

102

CHAPTER 6

Peter did not come. Andrew waited in the bar for nearly half an hour, then went into the dining-room and ordered lunch.

He took his time over it, but still Peter did not come. A feeling of apprehension grew in Andrew. Why did he not come? It could only be because he was being prevented, but why should that be? Andrew could not seriously believe that Peter was suspected of being involved in Rachel Rayne's murder, or in that of Magda Braile, if that should turn out to be murder. Yet after all, why should he not be suspected by strangers? And why, if it came to that, should he not be suspected by Andrew?

The fact that he had known Peter since his infancy and had read to him the works of Mina Todhunter, did not really tell Andrew much about what his nephew had turned into in his thirties. They did not normally see much of one another. Peter spent a good deal of his time abroad, and whether he spent it alone, or with friends, was something into which Andrew had never enquired. Vaguely he took for granted that there were women in Peter's life, but if Peter did not want to confide in him about them, Andrew saw no reason to probe into the matter.

Perhaps, he thought, he had been neglectful. He found himself beginning to wonder if it was possible that Peter had known Rachel Rayne before coming to Gallmouth. To take for granted that he would have told Andrew about it if he had done so was really rather presumptuous. And if Andrew now began to feel even very faint doubts of

Peter, why should the police not feel them too, somewhat more forcefully? If they did, surely they were mistaken. Yes, of course they were mistaken. But it might be difficult for Peter to prove that at the moment.

Andrew finished his lunch and got up, wondering if he should make his way to Barnfield House and find out what was really happening. He felt very restless, not at all like having the quiet doze that he was used to having in the afternoons. But he was doubtful about the wisdom of interfering in what was really Simon Amory's problem. If he could be of any use, he thought, he would have been sent for. But there was one thing he could do that might be useful, and if it was not, at least it would not do any harm. He went out into the hall, took up the telephone directory and looked for the address and number of Edward Clarke.

There were three E. Clarkes in the book. He prepared to dial them all, but at a second try was answered by the one he wanted.

Andrew recognized the high, thin voice at once, though all that was said was, 'Clarke speaking'.

'This is Basnett here,' Andrew said. 'I believe I'm speaking to the Chairman of the Festival Committee.'

'Ah, Professor Basnett – yes, yes, of course,' Clarke answered. 'What terrible things have happened since we first met. No doubt you've heard that they've found that poor woman, our dear Magda.'

'Yes, though I don't know much about it,' Andrew replied.

'Nor does anyone, I'm sure. Not yet. And perhaps they never will. I'm sure you know that of all the crimes committed only one in fifty is ever brought to the courts. Yet we're supposed to be a civilized society. Now what can I do for you?'

'If you aren't too busy at the moment, I should be very grateful if we could meet,' Andrew said. 'At your home, or your office, or here in the Dolphin, whichever suits you best.'

'Certainly, my dear chap, certainly. I'll be very glad to meet you again. And come here, if it isn't taking you too far out of your way. I normally avoid the office on a Sunday, and the press, which is massing at Amory's place, might track us to the Dolphin. After all, it's where Nicholl is staying. So if you don't mind coming as far as this, you'll be most welcome. You've a car, I assume.'

'No, but I can get a taxi.'

'Yes, that's the best thing to do. Well, I'll expect you in, say, half an hour. So glad to be seeing you again.'

With one or two more politenesses, they rang off, and Andrew picked up the telephone again and arranged for a taxi to pick him up in ten minutes.

Then he went up to his room to put on an overcoat, thinking as his eye fell on his copy of *Death Come Quickly* that when he returned from his visit to Edward Clarke, he really would settle down to read it. That was to say, unless Peter had appeared by then, or communicated with him somehow.

The taxi was punctual and with Andrew settled down in it, set off to the house called Rosemary Cottage.

It was no cottage. It was what is sometimes called a desirable residence, built probably between the two wars, with walls of white roughcast, a roof of grey pantiles and green shutters at the windows. The garden was very neat, consisting mostly of a wide, curving rockery. It was about three miles from the centre of Gallmouth, though the road to it was lined on both sides with bungalows. Perhaps, when the house had been built, it had stood almost by itself in the country, but now it was only part of a suburb, a prosperous one which had spread out to engulf what had no doubt once been a village.

Andrew left the taxi at the gate and walked up the short drive to the pale blue front door. The driver had asked him if he wanted him to wait, but Andrew had thought that the walk back into the town would not be too much for him. He rang the front doorbell and immediately heard footsteps inside the house. The door was opened by a girl of about ten years old. She wore very short shorts and a T-shirt and had a mass of tangled red hair hanging down her back. She stared at him wonderingly and said nothing.

Andrew said, 'My name is Basnett. I think Mr Clarke is expecting me.'

'Oh,' she said. 'Yes.' But she did not move aside so that he could enter.

'Perhaps if you would tell him . . .' Andrew suggested.

'Oh. Yes.' Her eyes were very large and a greenish brown.

'Tricia!' a voice called from inside the house. 'Tricia! Who's there?'

The child kept her gaze on Andrew for another moment, then turned and ran away into the house, leaving him on the doorstep.

A woman came hurrying to the door. She looked about forty and was short and plump, with a round, plump face and soft-looking features which it might almost be possible, so it seemed to Andrew, to mould gently into quite different shapes. Like the child, she had red hair, but hers was cut short across her forehead and all round her head so that it looked a little like a lamp-shade. She was wearing corduroy trousers and a brightly patterned jacket. Her eyes were friendly.

'I'm so sorry,' she said. 'Tricia shouldn't have left you here like this, but she's expecting some friend of her own and she's very shy with strangers. Do come in. Ted's out in the garden, mowing the lawn. It must be almost the last time he'll have to do it this year. Winter will soon be upon us, won't it?'

Chatting about Ted, the garden and the coming winter, she led Andrew into a sitting-room, a long room with

106

windows at each end, one of which overlooked the garden at the back of the house where Edward Clarke was to be seen on the lawn, puffing his way along behind a motor-mower. Like the child, he was in shorts and a T-shirt. The woman flung the window open, leant out and called, 'Ted! Professor Basnett's here!'

The first time she called Clarke did not hear her, the noise of the mower drowning her voice, so she raised it and called again. Her voice had almost the same shrillness as his. He stopped then in a startled way, switched off the engine and came trotting up to the house. He held out a hand to Andrew and shook his heartily.

'You've met Cecily,' he said, 'my wife. I'm so sorry to have kept you. I didn't really expect you'd get here so soon.'

Andrew was pleased to have it confirmed that the two were husband and wife, for they were so alike in their short, soft plumpness that he had wondered if they might be brother and sister.

'I'm very sorry to disturb you on a Sunday afternoon,' he said, 'but there are just a few things I'd very much like to ask you, since I've got to some extent involved in the tragic events in Gallmouth.'

'Of course, of course, I'll be glad to give you any help I can,' Clarke said. 'Sit down, sit down.'

As if it had been a direction for her, Cecily Clarke sat down in one of the plump easy chairs in the room. There were several, and a deep, soft carpet and a number of little round tables. Everything in the room was round and soft and cushioned, with almost no angles anywhere. It worried Andrew that Mrs Clarke appeared to intend to sit in on the discussion he wanted to have with her husband, yet there was nothing truly private about it. If she chose to join in it could do no harm. It was merely that her presence made Andrew feel self-conscious about his visit here, about its possible foolishness.

He began, 'I believe, Mr Clarke, you were acquainted with Rachel Rayne.'

'Acquainted – well now, that's a big word,' Clarke said. 'I'd met her once or twice. At that dinner where I had the pleasure of meeting you, for instance. We talked a little. But there's really hardly anything I can tell you about her.'

'Didn't she come to see you yesterday afternoon, in your office?' Andrew asked.

'That's just what the police asked Ted this morning!' Cecily Clarke exclaimed. 'And he'd never told me a thing about it. Wasn't that bad of him? The things I might think about him if I didn't know him so well. Go on, Ted, tell Professor Basnett what he wants to know.'

Clarke twisted his short, thick fingers together in a gesture of acute embarrassment.

'Yes, she came to see me,' he said. 'Only found me there by chance. I'm not usually there on a Saturday afternoon, but with the play coming off in the evening I'd stayed in town. I suppose it was your nephew who told you about his having seen her. It was he who'd told the police about it, so they told me.'

'Yes,' Andrew said, 'and unless they've dug up some other witnesses, he seems to be the last person who can say he saw her alive.'

'And the first to find her dead,' Clarke said.

That gave Andrew a very uncomfortable feeling. He said, 'So it seems. But what I want to ask you about is something that perhaps you'll feel you shouldn't tell me.'

'Oh, I know what it is, it's why she came to see me. And I'm not at all clear in my own mind what my duty is. I've never had a client murdered before and I've never thought out what, in the circumstances, I owe in the way of confidentiality. But the police persuaded me to tell them what I knew, which I must warn you isn't much, so if

108

you ask me the same questions I don't really see why I shouldn't answer them.'

'I may want to ask you some things the police didn't think of,' Andrew said. 'First, did she cast any doubts on the legality of her sister's marriage?'

'Oh, my goodness!' Cecily cried. 'You don't mean that! Why, those two were the most devoted couple you could hope to find.'

'People can be very devoted without ever having signed on the dotted line,' Andrew said. 'If one of them, for instance, was already married.'

They both stared at him with astonishment on their faces. Then Cecily shook her head vigorously.

'Oh no, I can prove you're wrong. Lizbeth once showed me a wedding photograph and there couldn't have been any doubt that it was of her and Simon. It was taken a good many years ago, but they'd neither of them changed much. And she looked so charming in her white dress, all lace and frills and holding a bouquet of carnations. Simon looked a bit grim, but then he always does, doesn't he? Perhaps I shouldn't say it, but I've never honestly been able to like him. But as I said, he was really in love with her, and the way he nursed her through that awful illness of hers was very moving.'

'Did she die here or in London?' Andrew asked.

'In London,' Clarke said. 'Simon hadn't bought the house here yet, but they used to come down to it quite often to stay with their friends. And it was very tragic to see her simply wasting away. Before the end she became the thinnest thing I've ever seen. But such courage! But what's given you the idea that she and Simon may not have been legally married?'

'Chiefly the intense interest Rachel Rayne took when Peter remarked that her sister had died intestate. After all, even if she was a rich woman —'

'Which she wasn't,' Clarke interrupted.

'Well, even if she had been, her dying intestate wouldn't have affected Rachel at all if her sister had been married to Amory. He would have inherited most of what she had, wouldn't he?'

'As there were no children, yes,' Clarke answered. 'If there had been he would have inherited the first two hundred thousand, and the rest would have been divided between the children. But of course, she never possessed anything like two hundred thousand and as there were no children he would have got all there was.'

'And her sister nothing?'

'That's right.'

'So you see why I'm so intrigued by that sudden interest of Rachel's in her sister dying intestate. Because I believe she would have got the lot if her sister and Amory weren't married. Wasn't that what she came to see you about yesterday afternoon?'

Clarke worked his fingers together as if he were kneading dough and puffed out his plump cheeks in a way that gave him a look of uncomfortable uncertainty.

'She never said anything about her sister and Amory not having been married,' he said. 'She simply asked if an unmarried woman died intestate, who inherited her property. I got an idea somehow that perhaps she'd had another sister besides Lizbeth Amory who'd died intestate, and she wanted to know what right she had to whatever had been left. But I admit she never said that definitely, it was just an impression I got. But if you're right . . .' He paused and gave a grave shake of his head. 'To think that we've known them all this time and never suspected . . . Not that it means much nowadays. They could quite safely have confided in us.' He sounded a little hurt that they had not done so. 'But of course, if you don't mind my saying so, Professor, you may be wrong.'

'Very likely I am,' Andrew agreed. 'I've only been trying to make sense of a small but rather odd incident.'

'But how could Rachel have found out about Lizbeth not being married?' Cecily asked. 'After all, there *is* that photograph. There *was* a marriage.'

'Which just possibly could have been bigamous, if Professor Basnett is right,' her husband said thoughtfully. 'How Rachel might have found it out, if she did, I suppose we shall never know.'

'Is this what the police came to see you about this morning?' Andrew asked.

'No, they only wanted to check that Rachel had been with me in the afternoon, and the time that she left the office. They asked me what she'd consulted me about, and I said the law governing intestacy and that was all. They didn't seem much interested in that. It was the time she left the office that they really wanted to know about.'

'Suppose, which I don't for a moment, the marriage was bigamous,' Cecily pursued, 'and suppose Rachel somehow found it out, why did she do nothing about it till yesterday afternoon? It doesn't really seem to me convincing. I think she was just a greedy girl who hoped there was something in it for her when she heard about the intestacy.'

'You may be right,' Andrew said. 'In any case, we certainly don't know the whole story.'

He left soon after that, after refusing a cup of tea, and started on the walk back to Gallmouth.

Two little girls came running after him as he let himself out of the garden into the road. They pranced along, one on each side of him.

'Are you a detective?' the one he had met before asked him.

'No,' he said.

'Then why have you been asking Mum and Dad so much?'

From that he deduced that she and her friend had been listening at the door of the sitting-room.

'That's quite a question,' he said. 'I wish I knew the answer.'

The answer, of course, was Peter. The last person to see Rachel alive, the first to find her dead. It was inevitable that he should be suspected.

By now it was possible that some other person, or even more than one, had come forward with a statement of having seen Rachel after her visit to Edward Clarke's office, and unless it could be proved that she and Peter had known each other before their visit to Gallmouth, no motive for his killing her could be suggested. But it was not necessary to prove a motive when it came to an arrest for murder. Undoubtedly it helped, but life could be made very frightening for Peter without it. So if Andrew could do anything to help him, he would certainly do it. The visit to the Clarkes had turned out moderately useful. It had helped to confirm in Andrew's mind certain possibilities that he had been considering, particularly since his visit to Mrs Wale that morning. Not that there was anything very definite about them, but they formed a pattern of sorts and that was interesting. He was so absorbed in it that he had almost reached the Dolphin before the bishop of Rum-ti-Foo began to bother him.

He found Peter waiting for him in the hotel. He was in one of the easy chairs in the lounge with a tea-tray beside him, and was just resisting the temptation of the cakes on the trolley that the nice-looking young waitress had wheeled up to him. She was just about to push it away when Andrew stopped her, ordered tea and chose a cake similar to the one that he had enjoyed after his arrival in the Dolphin, when no thought of murder had yet entered his mind. Its presence there now had not disturbed his appetite, however, and his walk had even stimulated it. There were not many other people in the lounge and it seemed as good a place to talk as any.

112

'Glad to find you here,' he said to Peter, settling in a chair near to his. 'What kept you?'

Peter poured out his tea.

'A statement,' he said. 'I had to go to the police station and make a statement and sign it. Where have you been?'

'Out to see our friends, the Clarkes,' Andrew said. 'But tell me, Peter, was this just a routine thing, or do you think they seriously suspect you?'

Once more the police were 'they', that faceless, anonymous abstraction.

'I wish I knew,' Peter answered. 'I think if I was them, I'd suspect me. But it's difficult to think of oneself in those terms. Why did you go to the Clarkes'?'

'To see if I could find out anything about the visit Rachel paid Clarke in the afternoon.'

'And did you find out anything?'

'I think so, though it was more or less what I expected. She wanted to know what the law governing intestacy was. But Clarke didn't seem to have asked himself why she wanted to know that. I think it was quite a surprise to him when I suggested that the Amorys perhaps hadn't been legally married. Mrs Clarke proclaimed that she had seen a wedding photograph of the pair, and if she really had, it leads one on to wondering if that marriage could have been bigamous. But of course, there was nothing definite in what we talked about. Perhaps their marriage was absolutely legal. I've only been wondering if there could be any other explanation of Rachel's sudden excitement at the information that her sister had died intestate.'

'You're assuming, of course, that she knew that the marriage hadn't been legal,' Peter said. 'How do you think that came about?'

'It could have come about in all sorts of ways, couldn't it?' Andrew said. 'It's possible that her sister married Amory in good faith. I don't pretend to understand why he should have wanted it. One has to assume that he'd been married very young, that it hadn't worked, and he and his wife had simply separated without bothering about divorce. And he knew that he couldn't have the Rayne girl without marriage, so he failed to inform her that he already had a wife. And then perhaps, years later, she somehow discovered the fact, though I don't know how. Perhaps his first wife appeared on the scene and made trouble. And then Mrs Amory must have told Rachel what she'd just found out. Didn't she pay a visit to her in America some time ago? Perhaps she told her then; in fact, it might have been the reason for the visit. Perhaps she wanted to discuss the situation with someone, because after all, bigamy is breaking the law, but if that's how it happened they must have decided to keep quiet about it.'

'You haven't any proof of any of this,' Peter said.

'No, but it could easily enough be found, by some investigation at Somerset House — that's to say, the place that's succeeded it, where they keep all the records of births, marriages and deaths. The question is, do I tell all this theorizing of mine to the inspector, or do I leave him to think it out for himself?'

Andrew bit into his cream bun and looked questioningly at Peter.

He wrinkled his forehead in a doubtful frown.

'You can't do anyone any harm by telling Mayhew about it, can you?' he said. 'The person who'd suffer by it if it was true is of course Amory, but if he can quite easily prove that he was legally married there'd be no damage done. So why not take Mayhew into your confidence?'

'That's what I feel myself until I actually think of doing it,' Andrew said. 'Then I think it would make Amory obviously the chief suspect, and I feel a sort of reluctance to do that.'

'You're forgetting he's got an alibi. He was playing chess with Mina Todhunter.'

'Who'd probably swear to anything he wanted her to.'

'Do you really think that?'

'Oh, I don't know. I don't know anything about their relationship. She may be the last person he'd want to find out about the bigamy and all. They're certainly close friends. I wish we knew why Rachel went to see her yesterday morning. What was the advice she wanted? I don't believe for a moment it had anything to do with writing for children, or even about writing at all. If that had been what she wanted, hadn't she Amory to ask, and you, who could have been much more helpful than Todhunter if what she wanted to know was a little about how to find an agent, or something of that sort. And having been given what she called a brush-off by Todhunter, she talked about wanting advice from me, didn't she? Well, if it was anything to do with writing, that hardly makes sense.'

Peter nodded thoughtfully.

'But have you any ideas about it?' he asked. 'Even wild ideas, with no proofs at all. I seem to remember you're rather given to that.'

'Well, as a matter of fact, I have,' Andrew answered hesitantly. 'It's simply that Amory never wrote any of his books. It's my belief that they were all written by his wife.'

'Good Lord, Andrew, that's wild even for you!' Peter looked really startled. 'Whatever made you think of that?'

'An address book that Mayhew showed me this morning.'

Peter gave a sigh. He leant back in his chair, stretching his legs out before him and crossing his ankles.

'Hadn't you better tell me all about it?' he said.

'It's what I've been wanting to do,' Andrew answered. 'You see, Mayhew wanted to see me this morning, and among other things he showed me an address book which had belonged to Amory's wife. He asked me to look at it and see if anything about it struck me. But before I could get around to doing that the news broke that Magda

115

Braile's body had been found and he'd no time to wait around for me to get to work on the book. He dashed out with a lot of other men, leaving the book with me. So I stayed where I was and studied it and found that under the heading "Typist", there was an address of a Mrs Wale in Linwood Drive. That seemed to me suggestive, and I set off to Linwood Drive straight away. I found it and I found Mrs Wale and had a talk with her and she told me that she'd typed two novels by Mrs Amory, which in what she called her humble opinion weren't much good, but that she'd never done anything for Mr Amory. Now what do you make of that, Peter?'

'Nothing in particular,' Peter said, 'except that in the last year or two of her life Mrs Amory tried her hand at writing, but without any success. Then some time after she'd died, Simon tried it and produced the remarkable best-seller, *Death Come Quickly*, but he didn't get it typed by Mrs Wale. In fact, he may even have typed it himself.'

'And after its extraordinary success he produced two fairly inferior novels which, it's thought, probably only got published because they had his name on them?'

'I believe that's correct. I haven't read either of them.'

'Well, that makes sense, but suppose you look at the sequence of events a little differently. Suppose you assume Mrs Amory wrote those first two novels, learning her craft as she went, and then something happened to her that brought that third novel to the surface. But she was a dying woman by then and though she finished it, she never did anything about it, didn't even get it typed and sent off to her agent, if she had one. And it lay in her drawer until some time after her death, when it occurred to Amory that he might see if he could get it published. But something made him send it off under his own name instead of hers. Perhaps he thought that publishers wouldn't look too favourably on a book that had been written by someone who was dead and couldn't produce anything more. But he may have done it fairly innocently, wanting it published in her memory as much as anything else, and it may be that the last thing he dreamt of was that he'd become a celebrity. But when it happened he couldn't bring himself to own the truth. It would have been too humiliating. If the facts had become known too he would have looked a selfish fool. So he's stuck to his fame and his fortune, his one problem being that he can't produce any more. He got those two first novels by his wife published, and both seem to have been failures, but now he's absolutely stuck, beginning to be thought of as someone who's written himself out and will never do anything more.' Andrew took another bite of his cream bun. 'Well, what do you think of it?'

Peter gave a sardonic little laugh.

'It's a good story, and I can't prove it isn't true. Whatever made you think of it?'

'You don't believe in it then?'

'I didn't say that. I'm only curious how you thought of it in the first place. I don't believe it came simply from reading that address book and talking to Mrs Wale.'

'No, I think I had my first intimations of it when I heard about those manuscripts in the desk in the summerhouse going missing. It didn't seem conceivable that Rachel was murdered to get possession of them. They couldn't have been as valuable as all that. But they could have been removed by someone who didn't want them to be seen. They were in Mrs Amory's handwriting, weren't they? Or at least two of them were. And if they were found, it wouldn't have been to Amory's advantage. He may have kept them ever since his wife's death out of sentiment, but with Rachel looking for them, as she obviously was when you had that glimpse of her running out of the summerhouse on Friday evening, they could have become a deadly danger to the famous personality that he'd built up.'

'You think Rachel knew the truth then about all this – or what you're inclined to think is the truth?'

'I believe so. I think it's the motive for her murder.'

Peter poured out more tea for himself, then sat back, frowning into space.

'Of course, you think Amory did it,' he said after a little.

'I haven't got as far as that,' Andrew said.

'But if you're right about all this, who else could it be?'

'I don't know.'

'Oh, come, Andrew, don't dither. Of course it's what you think.'

'There's still his alibi to be explained.'

'I thought we were rather inclined to believe that Todhunter would swear to anything to help him.'

'I think that's probably true,' Andrew said, 'but there's something about that alibi that shouldn't be forgotten. When I phoned her to get Amory's address, she asked me if I would like to speak to him. I didn't actually do so. I couldn't swear that he was there. But would she have taken a risk like that if he hadn't been with her? Suppose I'd asked to speak to him and he wasn't there, what would she have done? Said that he was so deep in his game of chess that she didn't after all want to disturb him, or that at just that moment he'd gone to the loo? No, I don't think she'd have risked it. I think he was there in the room with her when I phoned.'

'But suppose he'd only just got in. Suppose the murder happened rather earlier than we've been thinking.'

'It's possible.'

'And aren't we rather overlooking the death of Magda Braile?'

'Yes,' Andrew said. 'But I've had a feeling that we should deal with one thing at a time. Apart from anything, it seems to me probable that the two things are related, and that the murder, if that's what it was, of Magda Braile won't be solved until the other one is sorted out.'

'Oh, I'm sure that's right,' Peter said. 'In fact, it seems to me that the most probable explanation of it is that whoever shot and killed Rachel was on his way down into the town by that cliff path, the one that's hidden from the road by that grove of beech trees, and he met Magda coming up it on her walk and she recognized him, perhaps even greeted him, and was rewarded by being pushed over the edge of the cliff. In its way, that's simple.'

'Unless we're somehow thinking of this whole thing upside down,' Andrew said.

'Well, I think I'd better be getting back now.' Peter finished his tea and stood up. 'I'll phone you if anything of interest happens, such as finding those missing manuscripts. Did I tell you that the police are searching the house from top to bottom and they haven't told me why, but what it can be for if it isn't the manuscripts, I can't think. Perhaps Mayhew's thinking more or less along the same lines as you, though he doesn't want to talk about it. There's a way, you know, that they could prove a good deal of it if they could find them.'

'*Prove* it?' Andrew said. That had not occurred to him.

'Yes, if your Mrs Wale recognized them as the work of Mrs Amory, which she'd copied while Mrs Amory was still alive, and then she was shown the two supposed works of Amory that came out after *Death Come Quickly*, she could say who the real author was, couldn't she? Not that that would prove that he didn't write *Death Come Quickly*, but it would certainly cast a good deal of doubt on it.'

'Well, tell all this that we've been talking about to the inspector, will you, if he's still up at the house when you get there? If he isn't . . .' Andrew paused.

'Yes?' Peter said.

'Just let me know. I'd feel inclined to hunt him down myself.'

But once Peter had gone and Andrew was alone and had finished his tea his theory that Simon Amory had not written his three books began to seem to him absurd. For one thing, it took for granted that Amory was the murderer of Rachel Rayne, and that was something that Andrew was not yet quite prepared to do, though if he were to hear that he had been taken in for questioning by the evening it would not surprise him. It would, of course, mean that Mina Todhunter had taken a great risk in offering to let Andrew speak to Amory on her telephone, but perhaps she had simply done that.

'So there you are,' a voice said behind Andrew. 'I've been rather hoping I'd find you.'

He started round and saw Detective Inspector Mayhew standing in the doorway.

CHAPTER 7

The inspector came across the room to Andrew and dropped into the chair where Peter had been sitting. His big slab of a face had a sagging, tired look.

'I'm sorry I had to leave you so suddenly this morning,' he said. 'The news of the discovery of Magda Braile's body had just come in and I had to get out to the spot as quickly as possible.'

'So I supposed,' Andrew said. 'But I didn't follow you out for some time. I found that address book an interesting thing to study.'

'Because of the typist?'

'Mrs Wale? Yes. I went to see her, you know. I suppose we were both interested in her for the same reason.'

'Because of the possibility that she'd typed Amory's manuscripts for him?'

'Ah yes, I remember now that's what she told me you'd wanted to know. But I was curious actually as to whether she'd typed anything for Mrs Amory. Perhaps I ought to explain that.'

The big man massaged his knees with his heavy hands.

'Go ahead,' he said. 'I need a good many things explained to me.'

Andrew began to expound his theory about the authorship of the three books said to have been written by Simon Amory. In spite of his doubts of a few moments before, he found it surprisingly easy. It was as if his talk to Peter on the subject had been a rehearsal for what he had to say now. His mind had become much clearer as a result of that talk.

The inspector was an excellent listener. He hardly interrupted and when Andrew had concluded all that he had to say and sat there silent, Mayhew waited a moment as if thinking that there might be more to come. Then he nodded his head several times and gave both of his knees a slap.

'I won't say I haven't been thinking along the same lines myself,' he said, 'though I couldn't have put it so clearly. It came to me after we'd been to see Mrs Wale. I realized suddenly we'd only asked her questions about Amory, when the address book was obviously his wife's. There's no question about that. It has her hairdresser's number in it, and a dressmaker's, and even her sister's number in America, though that has become out of date, of course, since she's moved back to London. So it was a serious omission not to have asked Mrs Wale what contact she'd had with Mrs Amory. But I haven't had any time today to go back to see her. It's been one of those days. The removal of the manuscripts seems to me to be at the heart of the matter, and we've spent the day searching for them but so far without success.'

'What do you think about the possibility that Mrs Wale can prove whether or not Amory wrote his two second books?' Andrew asked.

'She can hardly prove it,' Mayhew answered, 'unless the manuscripts are found. It's only her word against his that she typed them for Mrs Amory. Of course, if she could produce some record of her work, some evidence like, say, a payment into her bank at the relevant time, it would help.'

'And what do you think about the matter of bigamy?'

'We're ahead of you there. We know it happened.'

'Amory was married already when he had that wedding photograph taken?'

'Yes, we've checked on that. It's quite clear. He married a woman called Mary Baker when they were both nineteen. The marriage broke up after a year and they don't seem to have thought a divorce was necessary. It's all in the records at St Catherine's House.'

'What put you on to looking for them?'

'It was almost routine. When events like the murder of Rachel Rayne happen, it's automatic that one starts checking on the relationships between the people concerned. We weren't expecting to stumble on bigamy, and when we did our thoughts naturally turned to blackmail. Was that the reason for the murder? We've no evidence of it, such as regular unexplained payments into Rachel Rayne's bank account, though there are regular withdrawals from Amory's. But he claims those have been simply to cover his normal running expenses. It could be true, though it indicates he lives on a pretty lavish scale. But perhaps he does. He's got lots of money, so why shouldn't he spend it?'

'But all the same, you're considering blackmail as a motive for this murder. Blackmail on account of his bigamy?'

'We're certainly considering it.'

'Or possibly on account of his having claimed to have written books, really written by his wife, and which were her property and so ought to have gone to her sister as her nearest relative, since her marriage to Amory wasn't valid.'

'Exactly.'

'Or possibly on account of both.'

'Possibly.'

'That would give someone a great deal of power over Amory. Enough to make him want to kill her.'

'Yet there's that alibi which you yourself, by that telephone call, help to confirm. Professor, would you do something for me?'

'Of course, if I'm capable of it.'

'It's to call on Miss Todhunter —'

'And try to get her to contradict herself about that alibi?'

'No, I'd be inclined to leave that subject alone. But I think you told me it was she who recommended Mrs Wale to Mrs Amory. So she knows that Mrs Amory was looking for a typist before her death. Could you talk to her a bit about that? I think you might handle her more successfully than I should. Find out what sort of person she thinks Mrs Wale is. See if she shows any special reaction at being questioned on the subject. Could you do that?'

'I could try. I don't promise results.'

'It wouldn't surprise me if you get some all the same.'

'Very well.'

The inspector left soon after that, leaving Andrew uncertain as to whether he ought to call on Miss Todhunter that evening, or could leave it to the morning. On consideration he decided to leave it till the morning and went upstairs to his room with the firm determination in his mind to make at least a beginning on reading *Death Come Quickly*.

He sat down with it by the window. His expectation was that he would fairly soon find that it was meretricious, pretentious, competent perhaps in a slick way, but unappealing to him. What else could anything be that had had the kind of success that it had had? Not that he set himself up as a literary critic and he soon found that he had been profoundly mistaken. The thing gripped him from its beginning, first with its skilled simplicity of style, then with the way its story was developed, then with its understanding of the strange collection of characters assembled in it. They were not a very nice set of people, and it was plain that the author did not think that they were, yet he had a kind of tenderness towards them which might almost have slipped into sentimentality, yet just managed to avoid it. The puzzle to Andrew as he read on was how this book, absorbing, moving, at times more than a little frightening, could have been written by Simon Amory. But if it had not been written by him, but by his dead wife, what kind of woman had she been? Someone it would have been fascinating to know, if she had ever allowed it. Yet possibly in meeting her the qualities that made the book outstanding would have been carefully hidden. If it was Simon Amory who in truth had written it, they certainly were. That aloof, rather grim man who seemed deliberately to avoid intimacy and friendship and who puzzled people by his apparent dislike of them did not reveal any of the qualities that Andrew would have imagined the writer of this book to possess.

He had read about a third of it before it occurred to him that if he wanted dinner that evening it was time for him to go downstairs. He laid the book aside and went down, going first to the bar for a drink. There was only one person in it. It was Desmond Nicholl.

Seeing Andrew come in, he turned away, as if he had no wish to speak to him or even to be recognized by him, but after a moment he turned towards him and with a smile that seemed to Andrew quite ghastly, as it would if a skeleton had succeeded in producing a smile, said, 'So you're still here, are you, Professor? I wonder what keeps you.'

'I wish I could tell you, but I don't know,' Andrew answered, 'except that I seem to have got involved with the police.' He ordered sherry, then carried it to where the other was sitting. 'It's not much use saying how horrified and how sorry I am —'

'No sympathy!' Desmond Nicholl broke in on him with a snarl. 'That's just one thing I can't take. I've been answering sympathetic questions all the afternoon. All I had to say to them could be said in one short sentence, but I've had to say that sentence over and over again till I've nearly been ill. If you've anything useful to say, say

125

it, but otherwise stick to the weather. I've been watching the weather forecast and it seems we're in for some rain. And a depression is coming up from somewhere. And an isobar is doing something. Do you know what an isobar is?'

It was plain that the man had been crying. His eyes, sunk in the sockets of his skull-like head, were red and their lids were swollen. It was also plain that he was drunk.

Andrew shook his head without saying anything. He knew the terror of sympathy himself. He had been through it when Nell had died. But Nicholl was not prepared to leave the subject at that.

'Well, what is it?' he demanded. 'Don't you know what an isobar is?'

'A curly line drawn over a map of the Atlantic Ocean,' Andrew said.

'And that's all you know about it?'

'Yes.'

'And you're an educated man?'

'So I like to think.'

'Well, I know more about it than you do, even if I don't know anything. It's a line on a weather map joining places with equal atmospheric pressure. *Iso* in the Greek means equal, and *bar* in the Greek means weight.'

'That's very interesting,' Andrew said.

'Fool!' Nicholl hissed at him. 'Don't you know I know you think I'm drunk. I *am* drunk. I shall remain drunk for as much of the time as I can organize it for at least a week. Magda and I weren't married, you know, though it suited us to say we were. But she'd been married when she was a kid and the fools had never bothered to have a divorce, they just drifted apart. And then when I suggested she might get ahead with one, even after such a long time, she said she couldn't because the bastard had got married again and she couldn't do it without his being

126

convicted of bigamy, and perhaps ruining his second wife's life. She'd a heart of gold, Basnett. Would you have done a thing like that in her place?'

'Probably not,' Andrew said. It was a matter to which he had never given a thought.

'Heart of gold,' Nicholl repeated, with tears in his voice. 'Not that it made any difference to us. Tell people you're married, they believe you. And in this blessed age in which we live, it doesn't even matter if they find you out. But I'd have liked to be married, I really should. I'd have liked the feeling of committing myself. But I don't think Magda worried about it much. Only when she met Amory the other evening, she couldn't resist giving him a fright. He didn't know if she was going to let the cat out of the bag there and then.'

'Have you told all this to the police?'

'*They* told it to *me*,' Nicholl answered. 'That man Mayhew's got a brain trapped away inside that great head of his. I don't know what made him think of it. I think it was something somebody said to him about intestacy. If Amory and his wife hadn't been really married the law worked one way, and a different way if they had. So he got that checked as quickly as he could, and checked up on Magda and me while he was at it. Not that that of itself is of much importance. What's important is that Amory had a very good motive for pushing Magda over the edge of the cliff.'

'Have they decided that is what happened?' Andrew asked. 'It couldn't have been an accident?'

'I ask you, how could it have been? D'you know that bit of the cliffs? They took me up there when the news first came in that she'd been found. The main road goes up a pretty steep hill from just outside this hotel and curves around the edge of the town, passing that blasted Barnfield House on its way, and there's a strip of woodland along the other side of the road. Then beyond that you come out on the cliff proper, a wide strip of turf with a path going up the middle of it. Well, it was still daylight, wasn't it, when Magda was there? Suppose she wanted to walk on the cliff, she'd have stuck to the path, wouldn't she? She wouldn't have gone creeping along the very edge of the cliff. She wasn't like that. What she wanted when she went out was a brisk walk in the fresh air to get herself stimulated for the show she'd got to lay on that evening. She'd have stuck to the path unless someone pushed her off it.'

'You think she met Amory on his way down to play chess with Miss Todhunter?'

'Chess be blowed!' Nicholl broke in. 'He'd just done a murder, hadn't he? And he went down into the town by that path beyond the trees because it's not much used and he thought he wouldn't meet anyone. And whom does he meet coming up that path but his own wife? She's going to be able to blow that nice alibi he's got waiting for him with Todhunter to pieces. So it's over the edge of the cliff with her. D'you remember how she said she was going to die in the winter? Nonsense, of course, and this isn't winter, but she didn't get it far wrong.'

'Do they know just when that's supposed to have happened?' Andrew asked.

'They're not committing themselves on that. They've that much sense. But they seem to think it was somewhere around four, or five o'clock. Personally, I don't think it can have been much later than four. She'd gone out for what she said would be a short walk and by four o'clock I was already beginning to wonder why she hadn't come back yet. I'd expected her by then, so it seems to me she must have been stopped before that.'

'Rachel Rayne was seen alive about three o'clock. She'd been into Edward Clarke's office to consult him about something to do with her sister, and my nephew, Peter Dilly, saw her come out of it.'

'So she can't have been killed much before three-thirty, and if I'm right that Magda met the murderer escaping from the scene only a little later, then we can put her murder down as having happened somewhere between three-thirty and four. Of course, it isn't important except for Amory's alibi. But I'm not the only one who thinks that Todhunter would sell her soul to help him and providing a fake alibi certainly shouldn't be beyond her. But I believe Mayhew will crack the thing in at least a day or two. He sees further to the side than most people. I've considerable faith in him.'

Andrew nodded, though just then he was wishing that he had not agreed to help the inspector by calling on Mina Todhunter and trying to extract from her some information about Mrs Wale. Even though the inspector had advised him to leave the subject of the alibi alone, it was inevitable that they should talk of it, and he would have to try to make up his mind whether Mina Todhunter was an honest woman or a shameless liar. He wanted to find her honest because of his memories of Mr Thinkum, and all the reading aloud of her works to the little Peter, which had probably laid the foundation of the very good relationship that had developed between them. Meanwhile, Andrew had to decide when to try to see Miss Todhunter. Should he telephone her when he had had dinner and ask if he could call in on her that evening, or should he leave it till the morning?

His decision in the end was to leave it till the morning and after the very silent meal that he shared with Desmond Nicholl who suddenly showed that he would much have preferred to be left quite alone he went back to his room, picked up *Death Come Quickly* and settled down to read. But he had not realized how tired he was. After a few minutes the print began to blur, his head sank back against the cushions, the book slid on to the floor, and Andrew found himself sailing in a ship at sea. The cabin he was in was a luxurious one, strangely filled with exotic flowers, and an open porthole gave him a colourful view of a desert shore, dotted here and there with palm trees. Then an exceedingly loud voice suddenly shouted at him, 'Rum-ti-Foo – All change!'

Andrew woke out of his dream with a start. It is a curious feeling to be wakened out of sleep by something in your own dream and it took him a moment to realize where he was and that his bed would be a more comfortable place than the chair for someone as tired as he was. He got up and began to undress and at last managed to get to bed and to switch off the light, all of which felt a great labour. Sleep came almost at once, and this time was dreamless.

It was at ten o'clock the next morning that Andrew entered Todhunter's Bookshop and asked the woman who was in charge of it at the time if it was possible for him to see Miss Todhunter. The woman disappeared through a door behind the counter and after a minute or two reappeared, telling him that Miss Todhunter would be glad if he would go up to her flat. He went through the door and climbed up the flight of stairs beyond it, arriving in a small hall with three doors opening out of it. One of the doors was open and he heard Mina Todhunter call through it, 'Come in, come in, Professor. So glad to see you.'

He went in at the door and found Mina Todhunter heaving herself out of an easy chair to come and greet him. She was in loose black trousers, a floppy yellow sweater and red bedroom slippers. She had apparently just finished her breakfast, for a tray with a coffee pot and a cup and the remains of toast and marmalade were on a table beside the chair in which she had been sitting. She gave Andrew one of the smiles that seemed to open right across her square face, showing her gleaming false teeth.

'I'll just clear this away,' she said, picking up the tray. 'As you can see, I'm not an early riser.'

Walking heavily, as she always did, she carried the tray out of the room into what he presumed was her kitchen, then returned and told Andrew to sit down and tell her what she could do for him.

'Because this isn't a social visit, is it? Not as early as ten o'clock.' She dropped back into her chair. 'You want something, and I hope I can be of use. Tell me, what is it?'

Andrew sat down. The room was a small square one which looked cosy and comfortable. There were easy chairs and a sofa covered in soft grey velvet, dark green wall-to-wall carpeting, no fireplace but a radiator that gave off a pleasant warmth, a table pushed away into one corner with a chessboard inlaid on its top, and pale green curtains at the one sash window. A newspaper was on the floor beside Mina Todhunter's chair, which she had evidently been reading over her breakfast.

She picked it up as Andrew seated himself and held it out to him.

'Have you seen this?' she asked. 'It's inevitable, of course, that they should make a lot of fuss about the death of poor Magda Braile, but they've linked it to Rachel's murder and really gone to town on it.'

'Yes, I've seen it,' Andrew said. He too had read the same newspaper over his breakfast. 'I believe, if it weren't for Miss Rayne's murder, they'd be inclined to think Miss Braile's death might be suicide. But it's a bit much of a coincidence, isn't it, the two things coming so close together?'

There was a quizzical look in her slightly bulging, pale blue eyes under their thick grey eyebrows as she studied Andrew.

'A bit much of a coincidence, yes,' she said. 'Now tell me what I can do for you.'

'It may seem a curious question,' he said, 'but I'd be very grateful if you could tell me what you know about a Mrs Wale.'

'Mrs Wale – good gracious, what has she to do with all these things that have been happening?'

'You do know her, do you?'

'I can't say I exactly *know* her. I've made use of her occasionally.'

'She's typed some of your work for you?'

'Yes.'

'And you recommended her to Mrs Amory when she wanted a typist?'

'Ah!' she exclaimed. 'Now I begin to see what you're after. But not really. No, I don't understand where Mrs Wale comes in. Could you please explain it to me?'

The trouble for Andrew was that he had not sorted out in his mind before coming to see Mina Todhunter how much he meant to tell her of his connection with Mrs Wale.

'Look, it's really Inspector Mayhew's doing,' he said.

'So I supposed,' she said, her gruff voice sardonic. 'I didn't think you could have dug Mrs Wale out all by yourself.'

'He'd made a slightly curious discovery,' Andrew said. 'He'd found an address book in the Amorys' summerhouse which was evidently Mrs Amory's, not her husband's. And the inspector showed it to me and asked me if anything special struck me about it. But before I could start to look at it he was called away because the body of Magda Braile had been found. So I was left alone with the address book and I took my time going through it, and something curious struck me about it. There was the name and address of a typist in it – Mrs Wale, Linwood Road. What, I wondered, had Mrs Amory wanted a typist for? And as I had nothing better to do, I decided to call on Mrs Wale, because I'd a feeling that she was what the inspector had wanted my opinion on. I thought he'd wanted to see if I found it a little strange that Mrs Amory had kept Mrs Wale's address in her address book. And I was quite right, because I found, when I saw Mrs Wale, that the police had already been out to visit her that morning.'

'Ah!' Mina Todhunter exclaimed again. 'I begin to see light. But go on.'

'Well, I asked Mrs Wale if she'd ever done work for Mrs Amory,' Andrew said, 'and she said she had.'

'For *Mrs* Amory?' she asked quickly.

'Yes.'

'Not for Simon?'

'No.'

'I see, I see. And so you leapt to the conclusion . . . Oh, how lucky it is that you came to see me, because I can sort this out for you. You leapt to the conclusion, didn't you, that the real writer of those books of Simon's had been his wife, and that he'd simply pirated them after her death. Isn't that what you thought?'

'I considered it, yes.'

'How sad, how dreadfully sad.'

That was not exactly the comment that Andrew had expected, but he wanted to understand it.

'I'm quite wrong, am I?'

She leant her head back in her chair and for a moment closed her eyes. Opening them again, she said, 'Yes, quite wrong, but I understand how you – and Mrs Wale – came to make the mistake you did. You see, when Simon first took to writing, his wife was already a very sick woman, and as they both knew, doomed. But she was still moderately active, and she took a great interest in Simon's attempts to write. So to give her something to think about and perhaps help her to keep her mind off her troubles, he took to dictating his works to her, instead of writing them himself. He's told me he found it extremely difficult. Dictating didn't come naturally to him. But it meant so much to her that he went on with it, and I believe it's

133

partly why those first two books he wrote are so poor. Partly, of course, that was first because he was learning his craft, but also I'm sure the dictating had something to do with it. And then, when the first book was finished, all in her handwriting, she came to me and asked me if I could recommend a typist. And I recommended Mrs Wale. That's the true history of Simon's pirating the work of his dying wife. What he did was done out of the most perfect love. Now isn't it sad that you should ever have thought anything else?'

Andrew did not reply at once. He sat thinking over what Mina Todhunter had just told him. She was watching him with a look of curiosity on her square face as if she were trying to assess how he was reacting to the information that she had given him. At length, as he did not speak, she became impatient.

'Well?' she said.

'Why did the murderer remove the manuscripts?' he asked.

'We don't know that he did,' she said.

'You mean someone else may have taken them?'

'I mean that Rachel herself may have removed them before her death.'

'Why?'

'Ah, why? Because she believed they were her sister's work and she wanted to prove that Simon was a complete fraud.'

'What makes you think so?'

'Something I haven't told anyone. You see, she came to see me on the morning of the day she died to ask my advice about what she ought to do with them.'

Andrew nodded thoughtfully.

'Yes, she came to you for advice, didn't she, and you gave her what she called a brush-off, I remember? And later you told me that the advice she'd wanted was about writing children's books. I didn't believe you, because straight after she'd been to see you she came to have coffee with my nephew and me and she started to ask me for the advice you hadn't given her. And no one would come to me for advice about writing children's books, or about writing of any kind. But she didn't get around to it, because my nephew dropped a remark about her sister having died intestate, and she immediately became very excited and left us. And it's seemed to me since it was because she believed that the books that have made Amory famous were written by her sister, and so should have passed to her, since her sister and Amory were never really married.'

'What?' Mina Todhunter exclaimed. 'Of course they were married. Whatever makes you say a thing like that?'

'I suppose you've seen a wedding photograph of them,' Andrew said.

'As a matter of fact, I have, but that isn't the only reason I have for believing it. Their whole relationship was – well, a married one. It was devoted, it was stable, it was secure.'

'I've no doubt it was, but it's possible to achieve that without ever having signed anything, or having taken any vows. And at the time of the supposed marriage I don't believe Mrs Amory knew that her husband was married already. He'd married when he was very young a girl called Mary Baker, whom you knew as Magda Braile, but that marriage collapsed after a year or so, and they separated without bothering about a divorce.'

'Good God, how did you pick up a story like that?' she exclaimed.

'From Magda Braile's second husband,' Andrew answered, 'though there I believe there was no actual ceremony. The two of them simply told people they were married and it never occurred to anyone to check up on them. It wouldn't, you know. But I suppose Amory couldn't get the Rayne girl without offering her marriage and so he conveniently forgot the existence of Mary

135

Baker. But at some time I think Mrs Amory must have discovered the truth. Perhaps Amory felt secure enough simply to tell her about it. And then I think she went to visit her sister in America to ask her advice about what she should do, because it's obvious that at some stage Rachel learnt what the situation was, or her sister's having died intestate wouldn't have meant anything to her.'

Mina Todhunter gave a deep sigh.

'Well, as a matter of fact, you're right,' she said.

'You knew all this, did you?' Andrew asked.

'Yes, ever since that morning when Rachel came to see me. She told me just what you've been telling me now, and I told her I didn't believe a word of it.'

'And didn't you?'

'I didn't know what to think, but I didn't want to get involved in the kind of thing she was trying to stir up.'

'Why did she come to you?'

'Because she knew I and Lizbeth had been close friends. She thought I probably knew the truth of the matter already. She thought I'd be able to tell her what to do about seeing that the credit for having written *Death Come Quickly* was given to her sister. And then that evening she was shot. And I suppose, like everyone else, I'd be thinking Simon did it if he hadn't been sitting in that chair where you're sitting now at the time of the murder. He's the only person with an obvious motive. Almost too much of a motive. It looks to me as if he'd been set up for the crime. Only someone miscalculated, because they forgot we always play chess on Saturday afternoons, and that suggests to me someone who didn't know me very well. Like Desmond Nicholl. Or a certain Peter Dilly.' She ended with a raucous cackle of laughter.

The sound made Andrew shiver slightly, but her face was solemn and anxious.

'Forget I said that,' she said in a gentler voice than he had heard from her yet. 'Of course Peter had nothing to do with it. What I'm actually inclined to believe is that the murderer doesn't belong to these parts at all. I think he may have followed Rachel down from London and had set off home again before her body had ever been discovered.'

'First stealing the manuscripts and pushing Magda Braile over the edge of the cliff?'

'Perhaps.'

'Why should he steal the manuscripts?'

'We don't know that he did. I'm inclined to believe that Rachel took them herself and hid them somewhere. That could have been quite a while before her murder. I dare say she could have got into the summerhouse some time before it and taken them and made a parcel of them and perhaps deposited it in a bank or somewhere like that.'

Andrew nodded. He remembered what Peter had told him of seeing Rachel come out of the summerhouse in the evening after the performance in the Pegasus Theatre. Peter had not said that she had been carrying anything, but anyway in the darkness he would probably not have been able to see whether or not she was. Then in the afternoon of the next day she had paid a visit to Edward Clarke's office. Might she not have left a parcel in his care? And if she had, had he mentioned that to the police?

'Well, I've taken up a great deal of your time,' he said, 'when all that I came to ask you was what you knew about Mrs Wale. But you've given me some interesting things to think about.'

He stood up. She stood up, facing him, solid and square, yet in some way on the defensive.

'About Magda Braile . . .' she said.

'She saw what she should not,' Andrew answered. 'Find Rachel's murderer and you've got Magda's.'

'Yes, I suppose so.' But she did not sound convinced.

At that moment they heard the door at the bottom of the staircase open and close, and then footsteps on the stairs. Then the door of the little sitting-room opened and Simon Amory came in. He seemed not to see Andrew immediately, but went up to Mina Todhunter, put his hands on her shoulders and began to shake her. His eyes were wild.

'Aren't you afraid of me, Mina,' he said. 'You ought to be, I'm a murderer, everyone knows that. So aren't you afraid of what I might do to you?'

CHAPTER 8

She showed no sign of being afraid. She looked up into his face with a melancholy smile, then withdrew from his grasp.

'In case you hadn't noticed, we have a visitor,' she said.

Amory swung round to look at Andrew.

'I beg your pardon,' he said, his voice suddenly low and hoarse. 'Scenes should be kept in the family.'

'Now what makes you say a thing like that?' Mina asked. 'You'll give Professor Basnett quite a wrong idea of the situation if you try to make him believe we're brother and sister.'

'Ah no, I'm only talking of the profound dependence we have on one another,' Amory said. 'Nothing as simple as a blood relationship. You see, Professor, I'm a little out of my mind, and Mina's the one person who can stop me going right out of it. The police believe I'm a murderer and I've just been through the worst couple of hours with them that I've ever spent in my life. They've almost made me believe that I could be capable of murder. And Mina's the one person who can convince me I'm not. Isn't that true, Mina? You don't believe I'm a murderer.'

'Of course you're not, dear,' she said. 'Now sit down and calm down and I'll make you some coffee. Professor, you'd like some coffee, wouldn't you?'

But Andrew declined it and since he was quite sure that they would not talk about whatever it was that Amory really wanted to discuss with Mina Todhunter as long as he was there, he took his leave, went downstairs and left

139

the shop. He then went to the coffee shop round the corner to which he had been with Peter and Rachel Rayne on Saturday morning and had the coffee that he had refused in the flat above the bookshop.

Sitting there, brooding on the talk that he had had with Miss Todhunter and on her explanation of how it had come about that the manuscripts typed by Mrs Wale had been written by Mrs Amory and not by her husband, he wondered how much he believed it and how much Miss Todhunter believed it herself. For a time he felt very confused and troubled, then he made up his mind to pay another visit to Edward Clarke, but this time, since it was not a Sunday, not at his home, but at his office. He did not know where the office was and had recourse once more to a telephone directory and having found the address, considered telephoning for an appointment, but then decided to arrive unannounced and take his chance of being able to see the man. Later he would go to the police station and tell Inspector Mayhew what Mina Todhunter had told him about Mrs Wale and the missing manuscripts. And then, he suddenly decided, he would go back to London.

He had not come to Gallmouth to become involved in a murder enquiry and provided that Peter was not in trouble, he did not believe that he had any obligation to remain. To be alone in his flat in St John's Wood, considering, now that all the work that he had had to do on Robert Hooke was definitely concluded, whether to begin another book on another noted seventeenth-century botanist, Malpighi, seemed to him attractive beyond words. He loved his flat and he always felt at home in London. He found it hard to understand now what had ever moved him to think of coming away from it.

Edward Clarke's office was in a Georgian crescent near to the centre of the town. A young woman greeted Andrew in an outer office and said she would enquire whether Mr Clarke was free. It appeared that he was, for Andrew was kept waiting for only about five minutes, then was shown into a room where Edward Clarke sprang up from behind a desk and came towards him with a hand outstretched and a smile of welcome on his face.

'The very man I wanted to see,' he said, 'but when I rang your hotel they said you were out and had left no information as to when you were likely to be back. But sit down, sit down, my dear fellow, and tell me what brings you.'

He piloted Andrew to a leather armchair that faced across the desk the chair where he had been sitting when Andrew entered, then he returned to that chair, rested an elbow on the desk and a plump cheek on one of his small, short-fingered hands and said, 'Fire away, now, fire away.'

Andrew wondered if he repeated everything twice to all his clients, and if he was capable of drafting a legal document without doing so.

'I've come to ask you a very simple question,' Andrew said. 'It concerns the visit that I believe Miss Rayne paid to you on Saturday afternoon.'

'Ah, that visit – yes, yes, I believe I've told the police absolutely everything that occurred,' Clarke said, 'but who knows, perhaps I didn't. You may be able to jog my memory about something. I find my memory becoming more and more treacherous. And the worst of it is, I still trust it. You see, when I was young it used to be almost infallible and so I got into a habit of relying on it. I hardly ever made notes of anything. I just trusted to that jolly old memory of mine. And now it lets me down at every turn and I still don't make notes. A bad habit, a very bad habit, that's what it is. The mistakes I've made because of it! But still, I think I can remember everything that happened on Saturday afternoon.'

'I don't think you'll have any difficulty remembering what I'm going to ask you about,' Andrew said. 'It's only whether Miss Rayne was carrying a package of any sort when she arrived here, and whether she left it in your charge.'

'I see, I see,' Clarke said, frowning as if even that question taxed his memory, and beginning to chew a thumb. Then he shook his head. 'She was carrying something, but she didn't leave it here. Now what was it? Oh, of course, it was just her handbag. A rather large one that was on what I believe is called a shoulder-strap. Would that be what you mean? But I can say quite definitely that she didn't leave it behind when she left.'

'Then I don't think it can be what I'm looking for,' Andrew said. 'And I don't think a handbag, however large, would be big enough to contain the things that have got lost.'

'Ah, you mean the missing manuscripts!' Clarke exclaimed. 'The police told me about them. They seemed to think that they may in some way provide a motive for her murder, that she was murdered to obtain possession of them. I can't see it myself. They can't have been valuable. But you think she had them in her possession, do you, but that she deposited them somewhere? Well, if she did, it must have been before she came to see me. But it's an interesting idea, very interesting. Of course, if she'd done anything like leaving them with me, I'd have told the police about it and handed the package over. I'm sorry if that's upsetting a theory of yours, but I really can't help you.'

'Well, perhaps since I'm here now, you can tell me why you tried to telephone me at the hotel this morning,' Andrew said.

'Ah, yes, indeed. Yes, indeed. That was because of a little theory of mine,' Clarke said. 'And first, can you tell me why our Simon invited your nephew down here to stay with him. I've gathered that they don't know each other well.'

142

'They'd met once when Peter was invited down here,' Andrew said.

'That was my impression. And of course that wouldn't be at all surprising if Simon was an impulsive sort of person, or just a sociable sort of person. But I think I'm safe in saying that normally he's neither. And as a matter of fact, our committee was rather upset about it. I don't mean that they were upset at finding that Peter Dilly was coming. Indeed not. They were delighted. But they were upset that the invitation had been given without their having been consulted. Very touchy, some of them are. But of course, they weren't going to upset the arrangement, and an official invitation went off quite promptly. After all, Simon *is* Simon Amory. And once they'd settled down to the idea, they recognized that Dilly was a great acquisition. Then we heard, when the question of booking accommodation for him came up, that he was going to be staying with Simon, so naturally we assumed they were good friends, knew each other well, and so on. And it was Dilly himself who happened to tell me that that wasn't so, that they'd just met once at some literary luncheon. To tell you the truth, I think he was distinctly puzzled himself at Simon's invitation. He seemed to feel that Simon actually disliked him.'

'Yes, that's what he told me,' Andrew said. 'But I'm inclined to think that that's an impression Amory may have a habit of giving people.'

'Yes indeed, yes indeed. I'm afraid it made him rather unpopular on our committee. And if he hadn't taken a sudden and warm liking to your nephew, why did he invite him down, particularly without having obtained the agreement of the committee? Why did he do that?'

'I haven't thought much about it,' Andrew said. 'Not knowing him at all well myself, I assumed it was just the kind of thing he was liable to do. He invited me to dinner without even having met me.'

143

Edward Clarke shook his head.

'Of course, I may be quite wrong about him, but I should say it was very unusual. And my little theory about it is simply that he invited your nephew in the hope that he would take his sister-in-law off his hands. I knew from Simon that she'd invited herself to his house for the period of the festival and I'd realized that he was quite put out about it. I didn't know why. I don't know now. But it strikes me now that it may have been to be able to hand her over to someone else that he had the sudden idea of inviting Dilly. After all, he and Rachel were much of an age, and he would have recognized that Dilly was good company. He could easily leave them to one another while he as usual went ahead with his work.'

'But do you think he did that?'

'Did what?'

'Get ahead with his work? It's only just occurred to me, but we've all been talking of three manuscripts having gone missing, but if he was going ahead with his work, there'd have been at least portions of a fourth manuscript somewhere in that summerhouse, wouldn't there? And if that – some unfinished portion of a new book he was writing – had been stolen along with the others, wouldn't he have been making a bit of noise about it? To have work you've spent weeks, or even months on, snatched away, must be quite the most upsetting thing that can happen to a writer.'

'That's true. Of course it's true, though I hadn't thought of it.'

'But perhaps he hadn't got as far as actually writing his fourth book. When he went to the summerhouse to work, perhaps he was still only thinking it out, plotting and planning, and making notes about it, which he may have taken away with him. Or perhaps . . .'

Andrew paused, very nearly telling Edward Clarke his suspicion that Amory had never written any of the books published under his name and so no fourth work had ever had any existence, but his talk with Mina Todhunter had left him feeling confused about the matter, far less convinced than he had been before it that Amory was a fraud.

Instead, he went on, 'You seem to think it's important that Amory should have invited Peter here without particularly liking him, just to help keep Miss Rayne off his hands. Why is that?'

'Why is it important?' Clarke said. 'Well, perhaps it isn't. It just occurred to me . . .'

'Yes?'

'Well, don't you think that the more we know about the relationships of the people concerned, the sooner we shall arrive at the truth?'

'Oh, certainly.'

'And Simon's relationship with your nephew has been a bit puzzling. But my idea makes it perfectly easy to understand.'

'And leaves Peter in the clear.'

'Exactly.'

'Well, that being so, I'm very grateful to you for having thought of it.'

'You're fond of your nephew, aren't you?'

'Very.'

'It's a nice thing to see. I've a nephew whom I haven't seen for over a year, and when he does come to see us, I'm quite afraid of leaving Tricia, my daughter, as you may remember, alone with him. His behaviour isn't, well, isn't exactly cousinly, and she's such a child, she doesn't have any fear of him. But that's just my suspicious mind at work. Parental jealousy, perhaps. I can't help feeling suspicious of Simon, though I haven't thought of any really sufficient reason for his murdering those two poor women. If his marriage was bigamous, as you suggested yesterday, I realize Rachel could have been blackmailing him. That's what her visit here may have been about, an attempt, perhaps, to raise her rates. All the same, to shoot her in his own summerhouse, wasn't that a bit foolish? Couldn't he have found a cleverer way of doing it? And with his supposed wife dead for so long now, would the police have taken any action about it? I doubt it rather.'

'I agree,' Andrew said. 'I don't really believe the bigamy in itself had much to do with it all. But now I really mustn't take up any more of your time. I only came to ask you that simple question.'

'If Rachel had had a parcel that she left in my charge. Well, I'm sorry I can't help you there. Nice to have seen you.'

They shook hands and Edward Clarke ushered Andrew out of his office.

He walked slowly back towards the hotel. When he reached the esplanade he paused, then settled down for a rest in one of the shelters along it and gazed dreamily out to sea. It had roughened up since the day before, though there was not much power in the breakers. They reared up their heads, curled over and came crashing down on the shingle, sucking a mass of pebbles out with them as the surf curled back once more into the deeper water. There was a feeling of moisture in the air, as if rain might be coming soon.

Andrew was startled out of his dream by a voice that hissed one word at him from the other end of the shelter.

'Murder!'

'I beg your pardon?' he said.

There was only one person there, an elderly woman, but so wrapped up in jackets and scarves that it was impossible to make any accurate guess at her age.

'Haven't you been reading the papers?' she asked. Her wizened face turned towards him. Her small, dark eyes peered at him with incredulous brightness. 'Nothing but murder in them. And when you try the television, there's nothing but murder there. All of a sudden Gallmouth's in

146

the news, because we've had murders here. You know that, I suppose.'

'Yes, I've heard a certain amount about it,' Andrew said.

'I should hope so! But it isn't just here, it's everywhere. Turn on the news in the evening, and what do you get? Murder! And bombs and civil wars and terrorism and child abuse and starvation. That's what the news is nowadays. And if it isn't that, then it's earthquakes and volcanoes and floods and fires. We're lucky, aren't we, having no earthquakes to speak of, and no volcanoes, and only an occasional hurricane and when they happen they're nothing much to speak of? We have a bit of flooding now and then, but nothing compared with what they have in other places. Oh, we're lucky, having only the few murders a week, and the deaths on the roads, and a bit of corruption in the police, so they say, to put up with. Aren't we lucky?'

Her voice had become more insistent.

'Yes, I suppose we are,' Andrew replied. 'We don't suffer much from natural disasters.'

'Ah, but we've got the Irish,' she said. 'Wouldn't you call them a natural disaster?'

'Perhaps we should.'

'Mind you, my mother was Irish, and a sweeter woman you couldn't find.'

'Which makes the tragedy worse.'

'That's right. It's all tragedy. The only kind of news people want is tragedy. I was going to a play on Saturday night that I was told was a tragedy, and I won't say I wasn't looking forward to it, but what happened? The leading lady got herself killed off the stage, not just on it like it should have been. That's tragedy for you. And the papers have been full of nothing else since. It wasn't like that when I was young.'

'Are you sure it wasn't?'

'Well, if it was, I didn't know anything about it. Now you can't help but know.'

'I think that's the point. It's all been going on since the beginning of time. Human beings aren't very nice people.' He stood up. 'I must be going. I've enjoyed our chat.'

But unfortunately the chat had distracted him and taken his mind off something that he had intended to think about. It was the first few words that Simon Amory had spoken when he had burst into Mina Todhunter's small sitting-room.

'Aren't you afraid of me, Mina? . . . Aren't you afraid of what I might do to you?'

At the time when Amory had spoken them, Andrew had assumed that they were ironic, that they were mere mockery of the possibility that he could be a danger to the woman. But suppose that had not been the case. Suppose he could really do her harm, and if Andrew had not been there, he would have proceeded to do it. What kind of harm could it have been? Not shooting her, not strangling her, not beating her to death. Yet why not? If he had already accomplished two murders, why should he not have had the thought of adding a third to his list? But if violence of that sort seemed improbable, with what kind of violence was he threatening her? Unless, after all, it was simply irony. Perhaps that was the most likely.

Andrew reached the Dolphin and went up to his room. He had just reached the door of it and had inserted his key in the lock when the door next to it opened and Peter came out.

'Were you looking for me?' Andrew asked. 'That's not my room.'

'No, it's mine,' Peter said. 'I've just moved in.'

'You've left Amory?'

'Yes, but I've been told it would be a good idea to stay around until the inquest. It'll be adjourned, but still I'll be needed, as the person who found the body.'

'Did Amory turn you out?'

'Not in so many words. He had his way, however, of letting me know that I wasn't welcome. So I thought I'd join you here.'

'I'm not staying. I'm going back to London.'

'No, Andrew, no, you can't do that!'

'Why not?'

'Because I want you to stay, I suppose.'

'There's really nothing I can do here . . . I've got to see Mayhew once more, but then I could go.'

'But you can help keep up my spirits. They need a bit of help. Mayhew seems to think there are only two people who could have killed Rachel, and one of them is me.'

'And the other is Amory?'

'Well, obviously.'

'I'm less and less inclined to think he did it. I've just been listening to an interesting theory that he invited you down here to act as a sort of bodyguard for Rachel. Or if it wasn't exactly that, it was a side effect of what he did. Now, let's go and have a drink and some lunch.'

They went down in the lift together. In the bar Andrew tried to explain what he had meant.

'I've been talking to Clarke,' he said. 'I went to him to ask if Rachel had been carrying any sort of package when she went to see him, and if by any chance she left it with him. You see, Todhunter, to whom I'd been talking just beforehand, put it into my head that Rachel herself might have taken those missing manuscripts and left them somewhere, and it occurred to me that if that had happened she might have left them with Clarke. But the answer was no, she hadn't and that if she had he'd have handed them over to the police, which of course I'd realized, but it just seemed worth asking, mainly to see if anything else came out while we were talking. And something did, though I'm not sure how important it is.'

'This thing about my being a bodyguard?'

'Well, what Clarke actually said was that he thought

149

Amory had asked you down because Rachel had invited herself, much against his will, and he wanted someone to take her off his hands. And that seems likely enough, but if it's correct, then it doesn't look as if at the time he was considering murdering her, because you were always liable to be around as a witness.'

'But if he killed her on impulse, that wouldn't have affected the situation, would it?'

'No, that's true.'

'All the same, I like the theory. I haven't been able to understand why Amory invited me, once I'd got over the idea that he'd done it for the sake of my charm. And it didn't take me long to do that. What else did Todhunter tell you? Had she any interesting ideas?'

Andrew told Peter as much as he could remember of his discussion with Mina Todhunter. He told him of her explanation of how it had come about that the manuscripts of Simon Amory's first two books had been in the handwriting of his wife and how it was she who had given them to be typed to Mrs Wale.

'And did you believe her?' Peter asked. 'Or do we stick to the idea that Mrs Amory actually wrote the books?'

'That's what I'm inclined to do,' Andrew answered, though with a certain reluctance. If what Mina Todhunter had told him was true, then Simon Amory was a man to be pitied and admired, not suspected of fraud any more than of murder. 'I'm going to talk to Mayhew after lunch,' he said. 'He wanted to know what I could get out of Todhunter about Mrs Wale.'

But when, about an hour later, Andrew saw Detective Inspector Mayhew in the police station, and had told him of his talk with Mina Todhunter the inspector appeared to lose his interest in Mrs Wale.

'I thought we had something there, you know,' he said. 'I thought that if she was shown those books that Amory had published after his big success, and if she recognized them as what she'd typed for Mrs Amory, we'd have proof that it was Mrs Amory who'd written them.'

'That's what my nephew thought,' Andrew said.

'But if there's any truth in the story you've just told me,' Mayhew said, 'that she'd written them to Amory's dictation, Mrs Wale's evidence doesn't amount to much.'

'Tell me something, all the same,' Andrew said. 'Suppose those books were really written by Mrs Amory, do you believe Amory would go the length of committing murder to prevent the truth about that coming out?'

The inspector cocked his large head on one side and gave a little grin.

'People commit murder for no reason at all, you know,' he said. 'If you feel inclined to do a murder, then you'll do it, motive or not.'

'And you've no other suspects but Amory, except my unfortunate nephew.'

'Oh, I wouldn't go so far as to say that. You see, we may have been looking at this affair back to front, so to speak. We've been thinking Miss Braile, that's to say Mrs Nicholl, was killed because she'd recognized the person who'd just killed Rachel Rayne coming away from the spot. But we don't know for sure, do we, that Braile was killed after Rayne? Suppose she was killed before. Suppose it was Rayne who saw the murder of Braile and who was then killed to silence her. You've got to look at a whole lot of different motives, haven't you? The books may not be of the slightest importance.'

'In fact, you're thinking of Desmond Nicholl,' Andrew said.

'The spouse is always the first person we think about. But we don't stop there. It's only a case of new avenues being opened.'

Andrew nodded and soon after took his leave. Walking back to the hotel, he began to think again of the attractions of returning to London. But he knew that he would not do this until Peter was ready to go too. In his room he settled down to reading *Death Come Quickly*. He was wondering, as he began, if he would still be as much impressed by it as he had been when he had started it. He was prepared to be disappointed, but instead it seemed to him to develop in depth and skill as he read on. But he found it more and more difficult to believe that it had been written by Simon Amory, that cold and arrogant man.

He started trying to imagine what his wife had been like. If she had written this book then she had been certainly very intelligent, very sensitive, observant and warm-hearted. Not that those qualities need have shown on the surface. Someone had said something about her being very shy and quiet. Who had that been? He could not remember for sure, but had a feeling that it might have been one of the Clarkes. Anyway, the Clarkes had known her during the time when she had been slowly dying, and perhaps had been writing this book and it seemed that they had never thought of her as a writer. Andrew wondered if the truth about the matter would ever be known. If Simon Amory stuck to it that he had written the book as after all perhaps he had, how was anyone to prove that he had not done so?

Perhaps Rachel Rayne could have done so, but was there anyone else?

Andrew went downstairs presently for his tea and his cream bun. But just as he was about to take the cream bun from the trolley that had been pushed up to his chair, he changed his mind and took a sober piece of gingerbread instead. Peter joined him there and chose a slice of sponge sandwich. It seemed to Andrew that he was looking older than he usually did. The events of the last few days seemed to have added several years to his age. Andrew wondered if the truth was that Peter was more frightened than he wanted anyone to know. To try to relieve him of some of the weight on his mind Andrew told him of Mayhew's

152

idea that Magda Braile had been killed before Rachel Rayne and that that made it possible that Desmond Nicholl was her murderer. Peter nodded gravely with an absent expression on his face, but said nothing.

Just then one of the waitresses came in and said to Peter, 'Mr Dilly, you're wanted on the telephone.'

Getting up and muttering something about who the devil was that, Peter followed her out. In a couple of minutes he was back again.

'Come on,' he said, 'we're going up to Amory's.'

'Why, what's happened?' Andrew asked.

'That was Gooch,' Peter said. 'Amory's manservant. They've just found Amory in the garden. Beaten up.'

'Beaten up — Amory?' Andrew exclaimed as he got to his feet. 'Why did Gooch phone you?'

But Peter was already halfway to the door. Andrew said no more until they were in Peter's car and had started up the steep road towards Amory's house. Then he repeated the question. 'Why did the man phone you?'

'Because I've been staying there in the house and he supposed I was a close friend of Amory's,' Peter replied.

'Did you tell him to call the police?'

'I did, yes, but it seems Amory told him not to.'

'He's conscious then.'

'Or was, for a little while. I told him to call the doctor and he said he'd already done that.'

When they reached the house they found that the doctor had arrived ahead of them. A car, which Andrew presumed was his, was in the drive in front of the door, which was open. But as they were about to enter, a voice called to them from the direction of the summerhouse and a man in a white jacket came running up to them. It was the man who had served the dinner on the Friday evening.

'He's in the summerhouse, sir,' he panted. 'I found him just outside it and I thought I'd get him inside rather than

153

leave him lying there. He may not know you. He didn't know me when I found him, then when I began to move him he suddenly come to and said what the hell did I think I was doing. So I said I was just moving him on to the couch where he'd be more comfortable and then I'd call the police and he said no, I wasn't to think of doing that. So I said I'd get the doctor and he said all right, do that and then he seemed to pass out again.'

'Any bones broken?' Peter asked.

'The doctor says not, but he's sending him to the hospital for an x-ray. The ambulance will soon be here.'

Andrew and Peter advanced to the door of the summer-house. Simon Amory was lying on the sofa inside, his eyes shut, his face of a deathly pallor except where a bright red mark crossed it from his chin to his temple, just missing his eye, and where a trickle of blood had spilled down from the corner of his mouth. He was breathing in a slow, snoring way. His collar was open and there were red marks on his throat. A tall middle-aged man was standing beside him, looking down at him.

Hearing Andrew and Peter outside, he turned to face them. He had a long, bland face and very little hair left on his high forehead, a small, puckered mouth and tired-looking eyes.

'I'm Dr Manton,' he said. 'I don't believe the damage is serious, but it'll make him feel pretty uncomfortable for a few days. You're friends of his?'

'My name's Basnett,' Andrew replied, 'and this is my nephew Peter Dilly, who's been a guest in the house for the last few days. He only moved out this morning. Do you know anything about what happened?'

'You'd better speak to Mr Gooch,' the doctor said. 'He found him and moved him before I got here. It looks as if someone thought of strangling him, then either lost heart or somehow got scared away. I think there was a bit of a fight first.'

'Oughtn't we to call the police?'

At the word 'police' the eyes of the man on the sofa opened.

'Don't do it,' he said in a hoarse-voiced, muttering way. 'I don't want them in on this.'

The eyes closed again.

'So he's conscious,' Andrew said.

'As conscious as he feels like being,' the doctor said.

'Who did this to you, Amory?' Andrew said.

He thought that there was going to be no reply, but then in the same growling way, with his eyes still closed, Amory answered, 'What's that to you?'

'Nothing very much,' Andrew said, 'but I'm curious. Was it Nicholl?'

'Why should it be Nicholl?'

'Only that he probably thinks you killed his wife.'

'Suppose I did?'

'Did you?'

'I'm not telling anyone.'

Andrew turned to the doctor.

'He's delirious, isn't he?'

The doctor nodded. 'Unless he's putting it on.'

'Have you given him anything?'

'Only an injection of a painkiller.'

Amory spoke. 'Ever been beaten up? First time it's happened to me. Changes the way you look at things.'

'I think we'll call the police all the same,' Andrew said.

'Don't do it, I say. I'm not charging anyone. All that's worrying me is why the hell he didn't finish the job. He had me by the throat and could have done it in another minute. Why the hell didn't he do it?'

'Do you want to die?'

'That's my affair.'

'I agree, but this would have been a messy way of doing it. And we're all of us getting tired of murder.'

'It wouldn't have been a murder, it would have been

155

an execution. I've paid and paid, but you can never pay enough.'

'Careful what you say now,' Andrew said. 'You're probably not quite in your right mind, so that protects you, but you don't want to start making confessions that you may regret later.'

'I'm not confessing anything. I'm only saying that in Nicholl's place I'd have done what he did, only I'd have finished the job. He's gone now, of course. Wherever he is, I hope he rots.'

There was a sound of voices outside, and of trampling feet. The men with the ambulance had arrived.

When they had moved Amory on to a stretcher and had carried him out, followed by the doctor, Andrew turned to Gooch, who had been standing waiting a little way from the summerhouse, and asked him, 'How did you find him?'

'There was a telephone call for him,' Gooch replied. 'It was Miss Todhunter. I put it through here, where I was fairly sure Mr Amory was working, but there wasn't any answer, so I came out to see if he was here or not. And I found Mr Amory and another man struggling here on the grass. I – I didn't interfere – I was just plain scared. But as soon as he saw me the man ran off. I thought at first he'd killed Mr Amory, he lay so still. But then he moved and said something, so I got him inside, and when I saw how he was hurt I called the doctor and then Mr Dilly, who I thought was a good friend of his, as he'd been staying in the house. But like I told Mr Dilly, he wouldn't have me call the police. Ought we to do that now?'

'I think we'll leave that to the people at the hospital.' Andrew took Peter's arm and started towards his car. 'Amory seems like a man who regrets the end of capital punishment. He sounds as if at the moment he'd rather welcome being hanged.'

'So you're sure he killed Rachel and Magda Braile,' Peter said.

'No, I'm almost sure he didn't,' Andrew answered.

CHAPTER 9

It surprised neither of them, when they reached the hotel, to be told that Desmond Nicholl had checked out. Andrew asked if he had left an address, and was told that he had left only that which he had given when he had registered on arrival. It was a London address, and made Andrew say that he had by no means given up all thought of returning to London himself, even if Peter found his presence here convenient. Peter only gave a laugh and said that he did not believe that anything would tear Andrew away from Gallmouth as long as the situation there remained as it was. Andrew knew that there was truth in that, though he believed that in the afternoon his desire to make for his home had been genuine. Some words spoken by Amory kept repeating themselves in his brain. 'I've paid and paid, but you can never pay enough.' Words spoken by a man in a state of shock, but perhaps literally true. Perhaps, on the other hand, simply a reference to remorse for an action he now deeply regretted. Or perhaps both. Remorse plus blackmail. It did not seem impossible.

It was not until the next morning that Andrew saw Amory again. He visited him in the hospital, after having found out which one it was by telephoning the man Gooch, with whom Dr Manton had been in touch. Andrew waited until mid-morning to pay his visit, finding Amory in a bed at the end of a long ward, looking pale and angry. The anger seemed to increase when he saw Andrew.

'Why the hell did they have to bring me in here?' he

greeted him. 'There's nothing broken, they could have sent me home. Or if they'd made up their minds to keep me here, why couldn't they give me a private room? Do they think I couldn't afford it? You were there yesterday, weren't you, when that fool Manton got the ambulance? I seem to remember you were there. I don't know what you were doing there and I don't know what you're doing here now. Can't you keep your nose out of other people's business?'

'I'm not very good at it,' Andrew admitted. 'I called in to ask if there's anything Peter or I can do for you.'

'Not to tell me I'd got to get hold of that damned inspector and tell him how I nearly got myself murdered?'

'No. I rather fancy that if I were in your place I'd be doing what you're doing.'

'What do you mean by that?' The snarl of Amory's voice grew rougher. 'What d'you know about my place?'

'Nothing much, except that I'm glad I'm not in it.'

'Oh, you're glad you haven't murdered two women and been beaten up by an enraged husband. That's very moderate of you. A lot of people would envy me.'

'Amory, if I can give you a bit of advice,' Andrew said, 'I wouldn't try to talk myself into being arrested.'

'Does it make any difference if I do or if I don't?' Amory said. 'They've made up their minds I did it, so why shouldn't I take a bit of credit for it? Get my picture in the papers. See myself on television going into the police station with my coat over my head to hide my face. Glamour, that's what I want. Haven't you ever wanted glamour?'

'If you really wanted it yourself you'd have called the police last night when you took that beating. But I understand you don't want them even now.'

'Certainly I don't. And I don't know if I much want you here either. Tell me, what have you really come for?'

'I suppose because although I don't think you

159

committed those murders, I think you know who did, and I'm curious what you're going to do about it.'

'You're going to warn me that if I know such a lot, I'm in danger. That's very fine of you.'

'No, I don't think you're in any danger.'

'Why the hell not?'

'You know that.'

'Not in any danger while that man Nicholl's around?'

'He isn't around any more. He's gone back to London. Anyway, if you think you're in danger from him, call in the police.'

'No.'

'You're in a very unfortunate position, Amory, I see that, but sooner or later you'll have to make up your mind what to do about it, and my advice to you is get hold of Mayhew as soon as you can and tell him everything. Not that I think for a moment you'll take it.'

'How d'you know I haven't made up my mind already?'

'It wouldn't surprise me if you have.'

'I'll tell you one thing I've made up my mind about. As soon as you take yourself off, I'm getting out of here. They want me to leave. If ever there were people who can make you feel unwanted, it's those bloody junior doctors. They seem to think you come here on purpose to make work for them, when all you wanted was to be left at home . . . Christ, look who's here!'

Andrew turned his head and saw Edward Clarke advancing slowly along the ward, peering to right and left at the beds on either side, looking, it was evident, for Simon Amory.

Andrew got to his feet.

'If you've other company, I'll be leaving you,' he said. 'I don't think they hold in these places with more than one visitor at a time.'

Clarke had reached Amory's bedside by then.

'Grand to see you looking so cheerful, Simon,' he said

mendaciously. 'I was expecting to find you next door to a corpse. Good morning, Professor. You're looking well too. I telephoned your house this morning, Simon, and was told by Mrs Gooch where to find you, but she certainly laid it on a bit thick. She'd hinted to me that you'd had your neck broken.'

'If it hadn't been for her husband being on the spot, I dare say I should have,' Amory growled. 'Why did you try to telephone me this morning?'

'Only to tell you that we had a committee meeting yesterday evening and we decided, in spite of what happened this time, that the festival has basically been a success, and we'd repeat the experiment next year.'

'What's that got to do with me?' Amory demanded. 'I'm not on your committee.'

'I thought you'd be interested all the same. You'll help us again, won't you?'

'Most unlikely. My guess is I won't be here.'

'You don't mean you're leaving Gallmouth!'

'More surprising things have happened. Why not ask Mayhew?'

'No, no, you don't mean that.' Clarke looked shocked. 'You aren't serious.'

'The question is, how serious is Mayhew?'

Andrew repeated that he was leaving. It seemed to him that neither man took any notice of this but in different ways were concentrating on one another. Clarke had a look of insincere cheerfulness on his face, Amory one of sneering contempt. Andrew walked away along the ward and out of the hospital into the street. He walked back to the hotel. He found Peter in the lounge, reading a newspaper. He put it down when he saw Andrew and asked him how his interview with Amory had gone.

'I didn't like it,' Andrew said. 'He seemed to be trying to draw attention to himself as suspect number one.'

'D'you think he's shielding someone?'

'I should think it's most unlikely. I put it down to vanity. I think he wants to build himself up as a murderer, and then at the last minute spring a surprise that clears him.'

'Such as letting on who the real murderer is?'

'Possibly.'

'Do you think he knows that?'

'I should say, almost for certain.'

'I believe you think you know that for certain yourself, Andrew.'

'Not for certain, no. But let's go and have a drink now. That interview left a taste that I'd like to get rid of. I'm sorry in a way that Amory probably isn't the murderer, he's such an unpleasant character.'

'Well, perhaps you're wrong. Perhaps Mayhew will come up with absolutely unquestionable proof that he did it.' Peter had stood up and the two of them were making their way to the bar.

To their surprise, they found Desmond Nicholl there.

He gave them a crooked smile and immediately offered to buy their drinks, saying, 'I suppose you didn't expect to find me here.'

'We were told you'd left,' Andrew said.

He had asked for sherry, Peter for gin and tonic. They carried them across the room to a table by the window. There were two or three other people in the bar who looked at them curiously, as if they were aware that these three were involved in the murders in Gallmouth, but were themselves too well bred to show their curiosity openly.

'I did leave,' Nicholl said as they sat down, 'but then I began to think what a damned silly thing that was to have done. If I'd hurt Amory seriously the police were going to pick me up quickly enough for grievous bodily harm and I'd do better turning myself in for it. So I came back to the police station and confirmed what I'd done. And I found that they didn't even know that Amory had had any trouble.'

'That's right,' Andrew said. 'Whatever his motives, he refused to have the police called in. I think he'd a sort of idea that you were justified in trying to kill him, thinking of him as you evidently did, or that at least was what he wanted us to think. He's a very unwilling patient in the hospital at the moment. I don't think he'll be there much longer.'

'No bones broken?'

'No.'

'Thank God for that! But what d'you mean by saying that he wanted it to be thought that he'd some sympathy with my action?'

'I'm really not sure,' Andrew said hesitantly. 'I've only a feeling that the man's such a complete phoney that one can't take any of his attitudes at their face value.'

'He's a phoney, is he?' Nicholl said. 'What makes you say that?'

But Andrew seemed not to want to answer that question directly.

'Perhaps I'm going a bit far,' he said. 'You're staying in Gallmouth, are you?'

'For the present.'

Andrew nodded thoughtfully, as if he considered this a wise course of action. After all, he himself had decided to stay. Reluctantly he had given up his intention of returning to London.

He spent the afternoon continuing with the reading of *Death Come Quickly*. How Peter spent it he did not know, but when he came downstairs for tea there was no sign of him. He came in presently, saying that he had been for a walk on the cliffs, the cliffs on the far side of the bay, not the ones from which Magda Braile had fallen to her death. Once he had said that and had ordered tea, he lapsed into silence, an absent look in his eyes and a slight frown on his face, as if the thoughts that had come to him on his walk were occupying him still. Andrew was quite content to be silent. His thoughts were on the book that he had just finished reading, wondering if it could possibly be really as good as it seemed to him. There was enough of the literary snob in him for him to feel that what had appealed to as wide a readership as this book had done must be second-rate. It was true that it was only as well known as it was because of the play and the film that had been based on it, but the germ of its popular success had been there from the beginning.

Peter interrupted his thoughts with sudden impatience. 'Well, Andrew, what *do* you make of it? You've had an afternoon to yourself. Haven't you come up with any profound ideas?'

'About the murders?' Andrew asked.

'Of course about the murders.'

'I haven't really been thinking about them.'

'Of course you have.'

'If I have, I've been leaving the job to my unconscious. Perhaps something very intelligent will emerge from it when I'm not expecting it.'

'You stick to it, do you, that Amory didn't commit them?'

'That's what I'm inclined to do.'

'Oh God, why can't you be definite about anything? Why don't you think he did? He seems to me the obvious person.'

'D'you remember something he said yesterday evening? He said, "I've paid and paid but you can never pay enough." What did that sound like to you?'

'I didn't think much about it. I thought he was wandering in his wits.'

'Well, to me it sounds like simple blackmail. There's a definite statement for you, if you want one. Of course, it could be a protest at some emotional suffering he'd had

164

to endure, but to me it sounds like a plain matter of cash.'

'You're sure, aren't you, that he didn't write those three books?'

'Pretty sure.'

'And someone else has known it for some time and has made him pay for it?'

Andrew nodded.

'But who could that have been but Rachel Rayne?' Peter demanded. 'And doesn't it supply the obvious motive for her murder?'

'Have you thought of Mina Todhunter?'

Peter gave him a startled look.

'Mina Todhunter?'

Andrew nodded gravely. 'Why not?'

'But she'd no motive for killing Rachel. And she's a friend of Amory's. And she's given him an alibi.'

'Or is it he who's giving her one? They alibi each other. Anyway, they were taking a risk with that alibi. If I'd rung up a bit earlier than I did and one of them, whichever it was, wasn't there, there'd have been a silence which it might have been difficult to explain.'

'I say, your unconscious is really working hard now, isn't it?' Peter said with a little grin. 'But it still hasn't come up with a satisfactory motive. I'm not sold on your theory.'

'Nor am I entirely,' Andrew said. 'I'd like to find something in the way of proof, and so far . . .' He stopped abruptly, staring hard at Peter, but not seeing him.

At that moment, just as it had happened the day before, a waitress came in and spoke to Peter.

'Mr Dilly, you're wanted on the telephone.'

Peter gave an irritated grunt, got up and followed her out.

After only a minute or so he was back, but in that minute his face had utterly changed. It had turned deadly pale, while his eyes shone with a shocked brilliance. He

165

stooped down to speak into Andrew's ear, to make sure that no one else in the lounge could hear him.

'Andrew, Amory has shot himself. He came back from the hospital this afternoon, seems to have gone into the summerhouse and shot himself on the spot. Gooch has just found him, and seems to want me there. Come on, we'd better go.'

'No,' Andrew said. 'I'm not going. You go and do what you can for Gooch. Mayhew can find me here when he wants me.'

It was not Mayhew who later that evening came to fetch Andrew, but a constable with a car. They drove to the police station where Andrew was taken into Mayhew's office. Peter was there with Mayhew and a sergeant who looked prepared to take notes.

'So we're to arrest Miss Todhunter for murder, are we, Professor?' Mayhew said, after waving Andrew to a chair. 'Do you care to enlarge on that?'

'First will you tell me if it's certain Amory shot himself?' Andrew replied. 'It isn't murder number three?'

'I'm not committing myself till there's been a post-mortem, but I think it's as certain as it can be,' Mayhew said. 'He let himself out of the hospital, took a taxi home, was seen arriving by Gooch, but did not speak to him, went straight into the summerhouse, not the house, and a few minutes later Gooch heard a shot. He went out and found Amory sitting at his desk, fallen forward, with a gun on the desk beside him and a sheet of paper there on which there were a few words, "I've done this because I deserve it." That was all. Gooch phoned us at once. I should say we got there not much more than a quarter of an hour later. He was shot in the temple and the blood was still oozing. I'm assuming that it was suicide and that he had his reasons, mainly that he couldn't live with two murders on his conscience, but Mr Dilly tells me that you've a different opinion.'

'That's so,' Andrew said. 'He had other things on his conscience, and as things had turned out his life had become for him a choice of evils, whether to reveal the identity of the murderer, which would have resulted in her taking her revenge by revealing him as a fraud who had built up a reputation for himself entirely on the work of his wife, a humiliation he couldn't face, or to remain quiet and let her get away successfully with murder. In the end it looks as if he was prepared to let her do that, since he did not name her in that last scrawl of his, but he couldn't face the idea of meeting her just as usual, playing his Saturday game of chess with her and incidentally continuing to pay her blackmail. He's only punished her by cutting off her regular income, the protection of which was her motive for the murder of Rachel Rayne.'

'This is very interesting,' Mayhew said, 'but how did you arrive at it, if one may ask that?' There was only mild sarcasm in his tone.

'I suppose it would be best if I go back to the beginning,' Andrew said.

'Usually a good place to start,' Mayhew agreed.

'Only I'm not really sure what was the beginning for me,' Andrew continued. 'I think it was when Rachel Rayne showed such a surprising interest in her sister's intestacy. It struck me then that that could only be if she believed that money or property of her sister's ought to have come to her. But that could only be if her sister had not been legally married to Amory, and also if her sister had had enough money to leave to make it worth Rachel's while to stir up an old scandal. The Clarkes, however, told me that they had a wedding photograph of the Amorys, so I began to think of bigamy, as you did yourself, didn't you, Inspector?'

'That's right,' Mayhew said. 'But I've been assuming

that the reason for Rachel Rayne's murder was that she'd attempted blackmailing Amory with the story of that bigamy. Why she'd waited so long to do it, because she probably learnt it from her sister on her visit to America, or perhaps even earlier than that, I didn't know, but it seemed to me an adequate motive for him to kill her. Only we'd very little evidence of it. Motive isn't enough.'

'I don't believe Rachel ever tried to blackmail him,' Andrew said.

'What was she doing in the summerhouse then on the Friday evening, when Mr Dilly saw her, if she wasn't looking for evidence of some kind against him?'

'Oh, she was looking for evidence,' Andrew said, 'but I think it was only because she wanted to put the record straight, not because in the first place she wanted money.'

'You think she believed her sister had written Amory's books?'

Andrew nodded. 'I think she'd had suspicions of it for some time. After all, she'd probably always known that her sister had tried her hand from time to time at writing, but had had no success. Then all of a sudden, after her death, Amory started writing and his first book was an amazing best-seller. I doubt if Rachel suspected anything amiss at first and as she didn't even like him, she didn't trouble to read it. But then perhaps she did, or saw the play or the film and something in it stirred a suspicion in her. There's a scene near the beginning of the book where some children go on a boat trip together and I can't help wondering – it's only a thought – if that scene didn't come straight out of Rachel's own childhood and couldn't have been known to Amory. Anyway, I believe that at some point something made her suspect Amory of pirating his wife's books so she came down here, looking for evidence. And she found it, three manuscripts in her sister's hand-writing in a drawer of the desk in the summerhouse.'

'And she took the manuscripts?' Mayhew said.

'No, I don't believe she did. She wasn't sure enough of herself. But next morning she called on Miss Todhunter, to ask her advice about how to handle the situation. She knew that Miss Todhunter and her sister had been friends, and Miss Todhunter was, or at least had been, a writer, with experience of the literary world. But Miss Todhunter only gave her a brush-off — that was Rachel's own expression for it, and straight after it Rachel ran into my nephew and me and we went to have a coffee together and she started to ask me for advice, only I gave her a brush-off too. That's to say, I didn't even let her get as far as telling me what she wanted advice about, but it was just then that my nephew dropped a remark about her sister having died intestate, and immediately Rachel's attitude changed. She became peculiarly excited and left us almost at once.'

'So she did want money after all,' Mayhew said.

'But not by blackmail. She wanted what she thought rightfully belonged to her.'

'Even more alarming to Amory, I'd have thought, than blackmail. It would have meant he'd lose everything he had, besides being publicly humiliated.'

'The person to whom it was alarming was Miss Todhunter.'

'Would you care to explain that?'

'Well, I believe she'd been living for some years on money she'd extorted from Amory because of her knowledge that the books that had made him so famous had been written by his dead wife. I don't know what proof of this she had, other than the fact that Mrs Wale, who'd typed them for Mrs Amory, could have said it was for her and not her husband that she'd typed them. But when I spoke to Miss Todhunter about this, she had a very ingenious and almost convincing explanation of how it had come about. But I think if you know what you're looking for, you won't find it too difficult to discover it. For one thing, I don't believe her own books have been selling for a long time, yet she's been living quite comfortably. Not luxuriously, she wasn't too greedy, but she appears to have had a steady source of income that enabled her to live quite pleasantly. For instance, her car is a BMW. Of course, she may have some other source of income, but I'd advise you to investigate just where it comes from.'

'If you're right,' Mayhew said, 'that income has now come to an end.'

'Yes, indeed,' Andrew agreed. 'She murdered to protect it, but things went too far and Amory couldn't stand the strain.'

'Even though what she did was in a way to protect him.'

'Yes, I wonder how often that's happened. I think it must be unusual for a blackmailer to murder to protect his victim.'

'But how do you believe she set it up? And that alibi – that wasn't very reliable, was it?'

'No, there she was taking a big risk. And of course she was relying on Amory to back her up, which but for that second murder I think he might have done, but that was more tha 1 he could stand. Of course, this is all most shocking gue ork, but I think what happened is that some time o' turday afternoon she telephoned Rachel Rayne, told h. he'd been thinking over the situation about her sister's books, and would like to meet Rachel in the summerhouse so that she could take a look at the manuscripts herself, then went up there to meet her, knowing that Amory would be out of the way, because he'd have arrived at the bookshop for his usual game of chess.'

'Queer to go on playing a friendly game every week with the woman who's bleeding you,' Mayhew observed.

'Remember, he was in her power,' Andrew said. 'He had to do what she told him, or that exposure that he dreaded so much could have happened. Well, I think Miss Todhunter met Rachel, shot her, collected the manuscripts and made off for the path down the cliff behind that strip of woodland. Perhaps she'd slightly disguised herself, put a scarf over her hair and dark glasses on or something like that, but on the whole trusting to luck that she wouldn't meet anyone. And she walked straight into Magda Braile. So Magda went over the edge of the cliff, and Miss Todhunter hurried home. And only a short time after she got in I telephoned. If I'd telephoned only ten minutes or so earlier I wouldn't have got any reply, because Amory wouldn't have answered for her and neither she nor Amory would have had any alibi. But she was just successful.'

'Do you think he knew what she'd gone out to do?' Mayhew asked.

'That's something we're never going to know for sure, isn't it?' Andrew answered. 'My guess is that he didn't know what she'd gone to do, but she told him when she got back, and warned him that he'd better back up her alibi, as she would his, or she'd expose him.'

'And what did she do with the manuscripts?'

'My belief is that if you get a search warrant and make a really thorough search of Todhunter's Bookshop, you'll find them hidden somewhere, perhaps in some attic, or under some floorboard, or somewhere your clever policemen will ultimately unearth them.'

'She may have burnt them.'

'It's possible, yes.'

'Well, I've found this a very interesting discussion,' Mayhew said, standing up, which Andrew took as a sign that the interview was at an end. He stood up too. 'We'll certainly look for those manuscripts in the bookshop, because if you don't mind my saying so, Professor, they're the one bit of solid evidence of which you've spoken. But I'm most grateful for all you've suggested.'

'I hope you'll find some of it of use,' Andrew replied. 'Good night, Inspector. Coming, Peter?'

They returned to the hotel in Peter's car.

Next morning Peter drove Andrew to the station to catch the 11.13 to Paddington. After all, he had stuck to his intention to return to London, though Peter was staying in Gallmouth. Andrew held that he had done all that he could there and would be of no further use. If it happened that he was needed, which he did not think to be likely, Detective Inspector Mayhew had his telephone number in St John's Wood.

He treated himself to first class on the train, which he did not often do. Usually, he believed, in these days first class was as crowded and uncomfortable as second. But there was always the chance that in a mid-morning train he would find a seat in a reasonably quiet carriage. He was fortunate, and found a seat at a table with no one facing him. Leaning his head back, closing his eyes, he let himself believe that he was just setting out on a brief holiday of peace and quiet.

Then someone moved into the seat opposite him and he opened his eyes to see what sort of a person it was. It was a small, slim, middle-aged woman who gave him a smile and said, 'Good morning,' when she saw that he was looking at her, but then settled down in her seat with a book she was carrying. It was a paperback copy of *Death Come Quickly* and she was about halfway through it.

Perhaps because she was small and slim and middle-aged, with brown hair turning grey and spectacles for reading, Andrew found himself thinking of the woman who he was sure had written the book. He had heard her described as shy and quiet and intelligent and observant. Of the shyness he knew only what he had been told, but of the intelligence and power of observation he was quite certain, but added to them understanding and compassion, as well as a sardonic sense of humour.

He thought of Simon Amory with deep dislike, thinking of how shabby a trick he had played on his dead wife, stealing her work, and on the public. Yet he did not feel sure that the woman who had written the book would have grudged him his success. It might even have appealed to her, partly out of generosity and partly out of amusement at the very success which she herself had probably never anticipated.

Andrew had brought nothing to read except a copy of the *Financial Times* that he had bought at the station and with which he was finished by the time he was halfway to London. He leant back once more and again closed his eyes. But he had no sooner done so than the lines that had bothered him during the earlier part of his stay in Gallmouth, but of which he had been free for the last day or so, when his thoughts had been much occupied with other matters, took a firm hold on his mind once more.

> *Among them was a bishop who*
> *Had lately been appointed to*
> *The balmy isle of Rum-ti-Foo . . .*

It clung to him all the rest of the way to London, and except when he was queueing for a taxi at Paddington, presently paying the driver and letting himself into his flat and looking round there to make sure that all was well, went on and on repeating itself absurdly in his mind. But once inside the flat he had other things to think about, for instance whether he should go out for lunch, or just go out to the delicatessen round the corner to buy some bread and butter, some cheese for his breakfast, some ham or some pâté and perhaps a tin of mangoes of which he was rather fond.

In the end that was what he did. He would go out for dinner, he thought, and presently, while he was eating the mangoes, it occurred to him that pleasant as they were, fresh ones would be a great deal better and that there was really no reason why he should not set off to one of the places where they grew. In fact, there was no reason why, if he wanted a peaceful holiday, he should not set off round the world. He had done that once before, but that did not prevent him doing it again, going perhaps in the opposite direction. And with winter coming shortly, it would be very agreeable to arrive in one of the places where they were just expecting summer.

After his light lunch he dropped into a doze in his chair, and then had a peculiarly vivid dream of Mr Thinkum, as he had never thought of him before, standing in a field with his battered top hat above a hideous mask of a face, with his muffler round his neck and his umbrella up over his head, with rain dripping off it. That the colour of the rain was red did not seem strange, only distinctly disagreeable. Andrew was glad to wake from the dream and make himself some coffee.

It was some days before he saw on the television news that an arrest had been made for the murders in Gallmouth and that the person charged was Mina Todhunter, the once famous children's writer. Since the news of the arrest had been broadcast there had been a greatly increased demand for her books. Naturally nothing was said concerning her possible motive. Peter had returned to London by then and told Andrew that he had been right about the hiding place for the missing manuscripts. They had been found under a heap of rubbish in the attics of Todhunter's Bookshop.

Another discovery was that the gun that had killed Simon Amory was the same one that had killed Rachel Rayne. It seemed probable that he had taken it from Mina Todhunter, though where she had obtained it was unknown. Just possibly it had been a souvenir that she had somehow acquired during her days in the ATS. As Rachel Rayne, like her sister, had died intestate and as she had no close relative, it would end with all the proceeds from *Death Come Quickly* going to the Crown.

Detective Inspector Mayhew had let on to Peter that he was hoping for promotion as a result of his solution of the murders. At the same time Edward Clarke was already making plans for an Arts Festival for next year, as the one this year had had so much publicity that he felt confident of its success.

By then a new and meaningless verse had taken possession of Andrew's mind. The bishop was forgotten. In his place, coming back from a travel agent where he had just been booking a trip round the world, beginning with Singapore and Australia, he started muttering to himself another jingle from the *Bab Ballads*.

> *'A very good girl was Emily Jane,*
> *Jimmy was good and true,*
> *John was a very good man in the main,*
> *And I am a good man too . . .'*